P9-CMR-417

His childhood friend in the arms of the enemy?

A black look crossed Nick's face at Meggie's news of her pregnancy.

"Don't worry, Meggie. We're going to make things right," he growled.

She shook her head. "When the father gets back to town, I'm afraid he'll want my baby, drag me through a custody battle." And she'd lose her child forever. "You know he can do it, Nick. His family has so much money and power."

Nick ran a hand through his hair, looking angrily around the town that hated him. "There's *one* solution, Meggie…."

There was *no* solution as far as she was concerned. "Thanks for the optimism, but I have no idea what to do."

Nick took a deep breath. "You can marry me. You can give your child *my* name."

Dear Reader,

'Tis the season to ask yourself "What makes Christmas special?" (other than a Silhouette Special Edition novel in your stocking, that is). For Susan Mallery, it's "sharing in established traditions and starting new ones." And what could be more of a tradition than reading Susan's adorable holiday MONTANA MAVERICKS story, *Christmas in Whitehorn?*

Peggy Webb's statement of the season, "The only enduring gift is love" resonates in us all as she produces an enduring gift with *The Smile of an Angel* from her series THE WESTMORELAND DIARIES. Along with love, author Patricia Kay feels that Christmas "is all about joy—the joy of being with family and loved ones." And we are overjoyed to bring you the latest in her CALLAHANS & KIN miniseries, *Just a Small-Town Girl.*

Sylvie Kurtz shows us the "magical quality" of the holidays in *A Little Christmas Magic*, a charming opposites-attract love story. And we are delighted by Patricia McLinn's *My Heart Remembers* from her WYOMING WILDFLOWERS miniseries. For Patricia, "Christmas is family. Revisiting memories, but also focusing on today." Crystal Green echoes this thought. "The word *family* is synonymous with Christmas." So curl up with her latest, *The Pregnant Bride*, from her new miniseries, KANE'S CROSSING!

As you can see, we have many talented writers to celebrate this holiday season in Special Edition.

Happy Holidays!

Karen Taylor Richman
Senior Editor

Please address questions and book requests to:
Silhouette Reader Service
U.S.: 3010 Walden Ave., P.O. Box 1325, Buffalo, NY 14269
Canadian: P.O. Box 609, Fort Erie, Ont. L2A 5X3

The Pregnant Bride

CRYSTAL GREEN

Silhouette

SPECIAL EDITION™

Published by Silhouette Books

America's Publisher of Contemporary Romance

If you purchased this book without a cover you should be aware
that this book is stolen property. It was reported as "unsold and
destroyed" to the publisher, and neither the author nor the
publisher has received any payment for this "stripped book."

To Mom and Aunt Mary, the hardest working supporters
in the world; and in memory of Regina Emig Ronk,
whose courage and advice still inspire me.

 SILHOUETTE BOOKS

ISBN 0-373-24440-1

THE PREGNANT BRIDE

Copyright © 2001 by Chris Marie Green

All rights reserved. Except for use in any review, the reproduction
or utilization of this work in whole or in part in any form by any
electronic, mechanical or other means, now known or hereafter
invented, including xerography, photocopying and recording, or in
any information storage or retrieval system, is forbidden without
the written permission of the editorial office, Silhouette Books,
300 East 42nd Street, New York, NY 10017 U.S.A.

All characters in this book have no existence outside the imagination of
the author and have no relation whatsoever to anyone bearing the same
name or names. They are not even distantly inspired by any individual
known or unknown to the author, and all incidents are pure invention.

This edition published by arrangement with Harlequin Books S.A.

® and TM are trademarks of Harlequin Books S.A., used under license.
Trademarks indicated with ® are registered in the United States Patent
and Trademark Office, the Canadian Trade Marks Office and in other
countries.

Visit Silhouette at www.eHarlequin.com

Printed in U.S.A.

Books by Crystal Green

Silhouette Special Edition

Beloved Bachelor Dad #1374
*The Pregnant Bride #1440

*Kane's Crossing

CRYSTAL GREEN

lives in San Diego, California, where she has survived three years as an eighth-grade teacher of humanities. She's especially proud of her college-bound AVID (Advancement Via Individual Determination) students who have inspired her to persevere.

When Crystal isn't writing romance, she enjoys reading, creative poetry, overanalyzing movies, risking her life during police ride-alongs, petting her parents' Maltese dogs and fantasizing about being a really good cook.

During school breaks, Crystal spends her time becoming readdicted to her favorite soap operas and traveling to places far and wide. Her favorite souvenirs include travel journals—the pages reflecting everything from taking tea in London's Leicester Square to backpacking up endless mountain roads leading to the castles of Sintra, Portugal.

THE KANE'S CROSSING GAZETTE

August 18, 1985
Delinquent Bombs Chaney's Drugstore!

*No injuries, but store is destroyed,
along with town's faith in foster care system.*

Chad Spencer, great-grandson of the town's founding father, Kane Spencer, told police last night that he and his friends never expected Nicholas Cassidy to set off a bomb during their night of fun.

"I swear on my great-granddaddy's grave, we never saw it coming," said the Spencer High School Junior Varsity quarterback. "All we were doing was hanging out, when old Nicholas whips out this space-age looking doodad. I'm telling you, that kid was no good from the get-go."

Cassidy, a resident of Kane's Crossing for merely one year, refrained from commenting as he was escorted from town. His foster parents were also unavailable for comment, but....

Prologue

August, sixteen years earlier

"Do you love me, Nick?" Meg Thornton asked, batting her eyelashes up at him as she leaned against his chest.

Fourteen-year-old Nick Cassidy felt his throat close up. They were hiding from the vile Chad Spencer behind a bank of rocks, wedged into the cool crevices, shaded from the Kentucky summer sun. In the distance, a riot of adolescent voices cut the air.

There he was. Chad, the pretty boy.

They were both breathing hard, and Nick could feel Meggie's twelve-year-old heart tripping against his arm. He moved his face away from the strawberry-tart scent of her hair. This felt weird, shielded from everyone else, huddled alone with Meggie.

As the voices drew nearer, she looked up at him with those big green eyes. Eyes like the center of a marble, clear and cool. Something to keep from the other kids after you tucked it into your pocket.

Nick had no idea what to say to Meggie. He didn't want to hurt the only kid in Kane's Crossing who treated him like a human being. And as if the youngsters weren't bad enough, the adults here—except for his new foster family and Meggie's aunt—also treated him like yesterday's trash. As if they could judge him after he'd lived here for only a year. Bunch of jerks.

Meggie sighed as she sat up, brushing at her fairy-wing-colored skirt, probably so she wouldn't have to look at him.

Man, he hoped he hadn't made Meggie mad. With the way her eyes had gone all puppy-dog sad, Nick knew he'd said something wrong.

He tore a piece of grass from the ground and stuck it between his teeth. "Don't get all mushy on me, okay?"

"It's all right." Out of the corner of his eye, he could see Meggie tilt her red head into the waning sunlight, the fading colors warming her face under a caramel-hued mask.

Town legend had it that when she visited her aunt in Kane's Crossing every summer, she looked more and more like a Gypsy, with her flared skirts and corkscrew-wild hair. No wonder some kids called Meggie a "witch." Not that she cared. She and her aunt Valentine, living in that creepy house on the hill, just laughed at the townsfolk.

"I hope Chad Spencer doesn't find us. I'm sick of his nasty talk," Meggie said.

Nick's hands fisted against his secondhand jeans.

"No worries, Meggie," he said. Footsteps stampeded on the bank above their heads, making his body tense.

A sharp laugh cut the air. Nick peered up, seeing a shadow crouched on the ridge above their rocks.

Chad Spencer's words flew at them like stinging stones. "Aren't you guys gonna French or something? Or doesn't the foster-trash kid even know how to open his mouth?" A chorus of mean-spirited giggles followed.

Meggie narrowed her eyes, dying to burn Chad with a comeback, no doubt. But Nick shot her a silencing glance. Spencer's beef was with him; the bully just wanted to make himself look good in front of her.

"Bug off," he said, using a glare he'd been practicing just for a moment like this.

"Oo-oh, so he *can* manage to form a word or two." Chad moved slightly, granting a slice of sunlight access to his golden hair. His royal-blue eyes glowed from the shade of his gelled bangs, and his turned-up alligator shirt collar lent him the plastic air of a Pez dispenser. "Are you tough enough to play Double Dare?"

Nick rose to his feet, holding out his hand to help up Meggie. She accepted the gesture, and the two of them stood, united, against their common nemesis. He hoped his silence was answer enough for King of the Creeps.

Chad stood, too. "If you want to prove how tough you are, meet me at Chaney's Drugstore tonight at nine o'clock. We'll see if your attitude matches my left hook."

He turned and tossed a smug smile over his shoulder at Meggie.

After the group left, Meggie touched his arm, her

eyes holding all the concern in the world. "You're not going tonight. Come over to watch videos with me."

Nick appreciated her easy-way-out alternative. Not many girls her age would understand a guy's need to save face.

But deep in Nick's heart, he knew where he'd have to be tonight. Facing Chad Spencer. Proving he wasn't just some poor little foster kid who had no business in Kane's Crossing.

Chapter One

October, present day

Meg Thornton stared at the man who'd just sauntered into her bakery. Six-feet-plus of leather jacket, cowboy boots and a frown.

"You chased off all my customers," she said, her voice barely above a whisper. She clutched the counter, wishing that the families who'd been snacking on coffee, lemonade and pie merely moments ago hadn't deserted her.

The stranger just watched Meg from behind a pair of sunglasses. She could almost feel his gaze running over her body—at least the part that wasn't covered by the counter. The sweet little secret growing within her belly was hidden by the Formica countertop and tiled wood, safe for now.

Meg shifted, wondering if her gray sweater had grown too tight during the last month, if he was looking at her slightly swollen chest, judging her as harshly as the rest of Kane's Crossing did.

When the stranger didn't answer, Meg narrowed her eyes at him. "May I help you with something?"

She eyed his worn jeans, the hole in one pant leg revealing a glimpse of knee. Her heart stuttered.

What if he wanted to rob her? Not that the cash register was full enough to even buy a new pair of pants, but she had house payments, a baby on the way. Any loss of money would hurt.

A faint smile lingered at the tips of his mouth, probably in reaction to her obvious confusion, but she couldn't be sure. At any rate, the specter of a grin disappeared, the tension in the room increasing tenfold.

Bitter aroma from a burned cake hung in the air, heavy as gunsmoke. Meg forced her chin up a notch, unwilling to be a victim of his intimidation.

Her voice was louder this time. "I'm not sure if it was you or the burned chocolate that killed the festive atmosphere."

The stranger took a step forward, scanning the room while his boots scraped against her floor. "Maybe it was your good mood that did the chasing."

His voice was low and gravely, the kind of voice that scratched down her skin in all the right places.

What was with this guy? In any other town but Kane's Crossing, she'd be afraid. Here, against the scape of her already tumultuous life, he was nothing more than a dark storm cloud. Her bravery increased in proportion to her anger. "Jeez, you cleared the place. Don't you have anything to say for yourself?"

He took another step, so close that Meg could see

the cleft in his chin, buried beneath a light dusting of stubble. A feeling of familiarity assailed her. Slowly, he took off his glasses, stealing Meg's breath away.

Eyes as hot as the blue tip of a lightening bolt. Pale, fathomless in their clarity. But why did she feel as if he hadn't doffed those shutter-like shades at all? He was no easier to read.

He just stood there, as if anticipating a reaction of some sort. Well, what did he expect? Maybe women all over the country sighed and collapsed at his feet when he *ta-dahed* and removed his glasses, but she'd never been one of the crowd anyway.

She used her words like a balled fist. "May. I. Help. You?"

This time there was a smile—a pensive tilt that lowered his gaze to his hands. Hands strong enough to break her heart in two if she was fool enough to allow him access. And that would never happen again, she promised herself. Not with *any* man, no matter how swoon-worthy the subject.

From a black-vinyl booth tucked into the bakery's corner, Deacon Chaney, the so-called town "loser," popped out his head. Great. At least some entertainment was being provided for her remaining customer.

The old man looked ready to shuffle through the stranger's ID and wallet. "Well, kiss my pink places," he bellowed. "You'd think this was the O.K. Corral here."

The thought of this stranger just strolling into her place of business and emptying the room with his gun-fighter stance irked Meg. "Listen. Maybe you're that heavy breather who takes great pride in giving me prank phone calls twice a week. Maybe you're just in here for a titillating little scare. Either way, you're setting me on edge, and I'm about to call the sheriff."

Yeah, as if Sheriff Carson would come running to her aid. He despised her about as much as the rest of this morally superior town did.

The stranger's gaze lingered over her every feature, leaving a trail of heat. The resulting blush swallowed the rest of her body in one languid flame. Meg's instincts told her to run to the back room and never come out again.

But she'd never run away. Not from this town, not from this man.

"You obviously didn't hear me when I said I'm calling the sheriff," she said, hoping he'd do the running.

The man actually laughed. Sort of. It was more like a chuff than an expression of mirth. "The sheriff in this place isn't worth fool's gold." He started to put his shades back on, then reconsidered and shoved them into his flannel-shirted pocket. As Meg stared in disbelief, he perched on one of the bar stools, leaned on the counter and ran a thumb and forefinger over his stubble. After a second, he laughed again and shook his head.

His identity balanced on the tip of her tongue, but she still couldn't place his face. She thought she knew this man.

She caught his glance once more and, after something jabbed her heart, just as quickly found a spot on the counter to stare at. Had she somehow caused the pain she saw in those startling blue eyes?

He looked so darned run-down Meg couldn't stop a rush of pity from overwhelming her. She wasn't sure how to apologize for misjudging him, so she poured a cup of coffee and set it on the counter. A peace offering.

Something was bothering this man, and the soft part of her wanted to comfort him.

Who was he? Maybe his familiarity came from the way he moved like a stream of mercury in motion. Maybe it was those eyes, the hurt. Hurt she knew all too well.

The stranger accepted the coffee, drinking it black and bitter. Meg backed away from the counter, crossing her arms over her chest, biting her lip. What could she say to this guy? Usually, she didn't have much trouble with small talk. She'd perfected it with the tourists who frequented her struggling bakery. The regular citizens of this town hardly bothered with her—not unless they wanted to poke some fun at the "town witch," the unwed mother-to-be who wouldn't give out the identity of her baby's father.

Much to her surprise, the stranger broke the tension between them. "Seen Chad Spencer around?"

The name jolted her. "Not lately."

When Deacon Chaney spoke up, Meg whipped her head toward the sound, almost having forgotten the elderly man was still in the room.

"Who's asking?" He sat on the edge of the booth's seat, his clothes hanging from his frame like rags draped over a scarecrow's cross.

The stranger hesitated. "An old…friend."

That voice ran over her body like a physical sensation. When had mere words ever been so sexy?

She shook herself mentally and tried to chase away the intimate air he brought to the room. "Are you from Kane's Crossing?"

"I don't claim this town." His jaw, cut like the edges of a steel trap, tensed. Snapped shut.

That was enough information for Mr. Chaney. "Chad's off cavorting in Europe, can-canning with the cream of the crop, I gather. Town's better off without him, I suppose."

"Don't say things like that." Meg didn't mean to scold, but you just didn't talk like that about the all-powerful Chad Spencer, high school quarterback hero of Kane's Crossing. All-state college player. King of the family's myriad of businesses. Pride of the town. Golden boy supreme.

Mr. Chaney pursed his lips and disappeared into the gaping black hole of the booth.

"Any idea when Spencer will be back?" asked the stranger.

Meg started busying herself, afraid to stand still, to give away the shaking that had started in the pit of her stomach and had coursed to the tips of her quaking fingers. She rattled around the dishes, not intending to answer the stranger's question.

She hated that she was so nervous. Nervous because she hoped her secret would stay hidden when Chad returned to town.

A blur of colorful clothing fogged the bakery doorway, causing the bells to sound like giggling children poking fun at the town unfortunate. Four men entered.

Sonny Jenks was the first to bare a tobacco-stained grin. "Woo-hoo! What do we have behind door number one?"

Junior Crabbe poked his grubby baseball-hatted head out from behind Sonny and his dirt-caked T-shirt. "We have us the town whore! Say, Witchy Poo, where ya hidin' that bundle of joy?"

Meg felt the stranger stiffen beside her. She hoped he wouldn't do anything rash; after all, she put up with this garbage all the time. She'd learned to live with it since grade-school summers, when these boys had followed Chad around the town like fungi on a heel.

"Junior, you're letting in the cold air," she answered, struggling for calm. "In or out. And if it's in, you'd better buy something."

Two more men leaned against the wall. Meg could tell by the way they weaved that they'd had a tipple or two in the bar down the street. One of the guys, Gary Joanson, stared at the floor the whole time.

Sonny scratched his armpit. "What do you boys think? Do ya feel like buyin' a magical cupcake from Chad's castoff?"

Meg couldn't stop the stranger as he bolted from his seat to loom in front of the good old boys. Sonny backed up. The stranger followed, causing the other man to cower against the wall.

Great. A rumble in the bakery. Kane's Crossing had hit the big time. "Now, don't do that, Mister—"

At the sound of her voice, the dark man peered over his shoulder and held up a finger, an emotional storm rolling over his features.

"Nobody talks to you like this, Meggie. Not now, not ever."

Meg was so worried about a fight starting that she almost overlooked one fact.

Only one person had ever called her "Meggie."

Aw, hell. Five minutes back in Meggie Thornton's company and he'd already said too much. That's the reason Nick Cassidy valued minimal conversation—you were bound to give out an excess of information at some point. And he liked to keep his agendas private. Very private.

The gutless wonder he'd pinned against the wall looked in need of a good cuff or two, but Nick wasn't about to start a row in the town that had labeled him a criminal so many years ago. He wasn't here to start fights with minions of Chad Spencer. He wanted the big boy himself.

Nick hovered closer to his new pal. "I don't hear you apologizing to the lady."

The man squeaked. Right. All talk and no action. Spencer's buddies were bravest when their fearless leader was around.

"Hey," Nick said, making sure a growl lingered just below his words, "I don't speak chicken. Did you say something along the lines of 'I'm sorry'?"

Meggie's voice called him away from his immediate anger. "Sonny, Junior, just leave, okay?"

Sonny and Junior. Nick remembered them well. Two brain-dead little teenagers who'd helped Chad Spencer in making Nick's life hell.

He clenched a fist.

Nick knew his temper was upsetting Meggie, and that's the last thing he wanted. Idiot. Why had he even come in the bakery? He should've just strolled into Spencer's Bank and gotten his information there. Meggie would never approve of what he wanted to do to Spencer. At least, not the Meggie he used to know, the butterfly who preferred skimming the high grass of distant meadows to giving Spencer the justice he deserved.

The cronies hesitated, then, with a nod from Sonny, they left with threatening glances. All but one, that is. The smallest guy lingered, then followed his friends.

Now that the trash had been taken out, Nick turned around to watch Meggie again. Hell, he couldn't get enough of her. Same stubborn chin, same ribbon-curled red hair, same marble-green eyes. Yet now, with the passage of years, her chin seemed lowered, her hair a less vibrant shade, her eyes clouded with a pain he wanted to brush away. And her willowy body, once so free and spirited, wasn't the same. The Meggie he knew had never worn baggy gray sweaters. Her evident loss of childlike wonder clutched at his heart, but he was experiencing a totally different, unexpected feeling at the same time. A pull, a pounding in his belly. More than the innocent companionship a summer friend had felt.

He averted his gaze from her, thinking he had no right to feel anything for Meggie. She no doubt remembered a fourteen-year-old boy who'd been thrown out of town for bombing Chaney's Drugstore. Why would she possibly welcome him back to Kane's Crossing?

And, most important of all, he wondered what those cronies had meant by calling her "Chad's castoff."

Nick hoped to God it didn't mean what he thought it did. He wasn't sure he could stand the thought of his childhood friend in the arms of the enemy.

When he turned back to her, Meggie was shaking her head, fists propped on her hips. Nick felt a powerful heat steal through his body at this glimpse of her returning feistiness.

She said, "I can't believe this."

He ducked his head, feeling like a dog being reprimanded for chasing skunks. "Sorry, ma'am." Maybe he could play this down, just leave, pretend as though he'd never stood outside the bakery, staring at the sign, wishing he could see Meggie again.

"Nick Cassidy?"

Her voice broke on the end of his last name. It wasn't the one he'd been born with, but who the hell cared. He'd located his real parents years ago, and the disappointment of their reality still ripped his self-respect to shreds every time he thought about it.

A haunted shade cooled Meggie's gaze. He'd give anything—the millions of dollars he'd made from his ridiculously successful business ventures, even the shirt off his back—to still her sadness. Usually, words rammed against his lips, anxious to escape from the prison of his mind. But, right now, he was truly speechless, and the silence weighing over their heads felt even more oppressive.

He wanted to walk to her, run his thumb over her soft-looking skin, trace the light freckles he remembered. He wondered if she still had those playful flecks of color on her cheeks. If he could just get close enough to smell the strawberry-tart scent he remembered so well, he'd be able to see for himself. But he didn't dare. Best to just leave.

Nick started to turn around, to exit the bakery and make Meggie a distant memory, but the elderly man from the corner booth blocked his way. He seemed so familiar...

"Cassidy?" the man asked, watery eyes intense with a purpose Nick didn't understand.

Nick fit his thumbs into the belt loops of his jeans. It was habit. An I-don't-give-a-hoot gesture he'd perfected through the journey of too many foster homes.

The old man's mouth twitched, then he grunted and

left the building. The bells echoed through the air, mocking Nick with their laughter.

"That was Mr. Chaney," said Meggie. "You probably remember him."

Was that accusation in her voice? Of course. When they'd hauled him out of town, with Spencer and his buddies snickering behind the sight of red-and-blue cop car lights, Nick had never gotten the chance to talk to anyone—not his foster mom or dad…not even their son, Sam.

Or Meggie.

He'd never been able to explain that Spencer had invited him to Chaney's Drugstore to fight, but, instead, had set off a homemade bomb. Everyone in Kane's Crossing had believed Spencer when he accused Nick of exploding the device. Nick had been there, he'd seen it destroy the building, and who was going to believe the rantings of the town hard-luck case when the town golden boy was accusing him of a crime?

His foster parents had been so sick with disappointment, they'd refused to see him; they'd even called off their plans to adopt him into their family. Even Sam, whom Nick had just about worshiped with a younger foster brother's devotion, had refrained from contacting him. The state of Kentucky had moved Nick to another home after he'd served some time in a juvenile delinquent facility.

But now he was back in town to right some wrongs. The car crash he'd lived through mere months ago had given him some perspective, had made him realize that there was a little town in the middle of America that still thought the worst of him. He couldn't live with himself knowing that he'd never erased this falsehood.

Clearing his name and serving justice to Spencer on one of his own silver spoons became top priority.

He gritted his teeth. What the hell, Meggie deserved at least some explanation. "I see this place hasn't forgotten my name."

"How could they? You're an urban legend in a provincial town. Almost a celebrity."

Her tone teetered on the edge of sarcasm, and his crusade against Spencer increased twofold. Even Meggie had been infected by Spencer's lies. Nick felt something in the area of his heart crack, but he stiffened his jaw and narrowed his eyes to fight the feeling. "You've made up your mind."

Meggie's eyes flashed, and she stepped to the end of the counter. For the first time, Nick saw the slight roundness of her stomach. He felt the wind get knocked out of him.

Do ya feel like buyin' a magical cupcake from Chad's castoff?

Say, Witchy Poo, where ya hidin' that bundle of joy?

Dear, God, please have him be wrong.

She said, "It's pretty easy to form an opinion over the course of years. Have you finally come back to explain yourself, Nick?"

Explain *himself?* He didn't play the explaining game. "Whatever I have to say would fall on deaf ears." He couldn't stop his gaze from straying to her belly.

A short laugh cut the air when she noticed his scrutiny. "Oh, great. You're curious, too. Don't even ask."

He kept his mouth shut. It's what he knew how to do best, and it frequently kept him out of more trouble than he was worth.

"So?" She reached up to skim a red curl away from

the corner of an eye, but she couldn't hide the tremble of her finger. "Why did you come back?"

Why? Because he wanted to see justice done. Because he wanted to find his foster family, to see if they'd come to forgive him for a crime he didn't commit in the first place.

Yes, he was guilty of never trying to contact them—their rejection had stung too much the first time to give them another chance to hurt him again—but surely the passage of years had lent them some sense of leniency.

He clenched his jaw, unwilling to answer her simple question. *Simple.* He almost laughed at the word. Nothing was ever simple.

Meggie chuckled, but the accompanying smile was far from happy. "I assume your return has something to do with your childhood buddy. Why are you looking for Chad?"

She'd whispered the name, but somehow it seemed to crash through the room like a wrecking ball. "No reason."

"Right."

He didn't want it to be like this with Meggie. He wanted summer rains experienced from the shelter of a small cave. He wanted cool dips in the local swimming hole and long talks about the future as the sun braided the sky into a bluish-orange sunset. He wanted the girl who laughed in the face of anyone who dared call her "Witchy Poo." But that girl was gone.

Meggie sighed, and he related to her frustration. He'd never suffered a tied tongue around her because she'd always understood him.

"Have you gone by your old home?"

Evidently, she'd given up her attempt to wheedle information out of him. "No one was there."

"It's too bad, you know. It used to be such a neat house, all comfy with those flower beds and the huge lawn. Now it's just…"

Her eyes had gone all dark, almost like water from a Venetian canal, littered with so much beneath the surface. In all his travels, weighed by a rucksack and too many painful memories, he'd never seen a green like Meggie's eyes. He'd done his damnedest to erase his memories after he'd earned his way through college, crossing Europe in second-class train cars, crashing night after night in youth hostels. But instead of filling his head with the beauty of new experiences, his adventures had only succeeded in feeding his hate for Spencer. After all, he'd never have run away from his real world if he hadn't been thrown out in the first place.

All those roads he'd walked only led to one place—Kane's Crossing. Back to a tiny, loving home he'd lived in for one shining year, enough time to know he was capable of having a chance to be loved by foster parents and a brother who would've hung the moon for his younger sibling.

He rehooked his thumbs in his belt loops. "What do you mean my house 'used to be' so cozy?"

"You don't know?" Her eyes widened, teared up.

Nick shook his head, steeling himself for bad news.

"I thought somehow someone would've told you. Your foster parents died about five years ago."

It felt as if an invisible force had jump-kicked him square in the chest. Stunned, he could only think to look away, to hide the pain he knew was marking his face like a bloody wound. Gone? He'd always meant to come back someday, to thank his foster parents for their glimmer of hope and acceptance. And now it was too late.

"How?" He hoped to God his voice had come out strong.

She paused. "There was an accident at the Spencer Factory. After your dad died there, your mom carried on for about a year longer. Then she caught pneumonia and—"

He held up a hand, stopping her explanation. Why had he asked for details? He should've known their deaths had something to do with Chad Spencer. The man dirtied every portion of Nick's life.

Spencer would pay for this. In blood, if need be.

Meggie continued. "And I don't know about Sam. Nobody's heard from him since he left town. Some people say he became a cop in Washington, D.C., got married." She paused. "He had steel in his eyes after your parents died. He blamed the Spencer Factory."

So Sam was bitter, too. Nick remembered spending long nights with his foster brother, sitting on the roof of their home, talking about a world filled with beautiful girls and fast cars.

Maybe Sam would've even supported the plan Nick had created to ruin Chad Spencer's life. He wished he could see his foster brother's crooked grin again, to draw strength from its sticks-and-stones-may-break-my-bones slant.

He swallowed, collected himself for a moment. Hands fisting, he nodded at her rounded belly. "Are you carrying Spencer's child?"

"That's none of your damned business." She stepped behind the counter again, grabbing a nearby cloth to wipe down the Formica counter. "It was great seeing you again, Nick. Feel free to leave."

He stood there for a moment, wondering if he should let down his guard, explain to her why he was back in town. He wanted to ask if she'd married Spencer, but, from the sound of the teasing he'd heard earlier, he knew that wasn't the case. In all likelihood, Meggie was going to be a single mother.

She'd betrayed Nick without even realizing it.

He waited for Meggie to say something else. Anything. Yet, except for the friction of cloth on the counter, there was only silence.

Nick slipped on his shades and walked toward Meggie. Her eyes grew wide, and she froze. Her fear felt like a slap to his ego. She'd never looked at him with wariness before today.

To hell with it. Why should he care if she'd gotten herself in trouble with a scumbag like Spencer? She was a big girl now, old enough to take care of her problems without Nick Cassidy galloping to her rescue.

He reached into his pocket and tossed the contents by her wash rag. A pile of bills. "For all the people my attitude chased out," he said, turning around to leave.

She didn't stop him, not that Nick expected her to. Coming into the bakery had been a bad idea, because now he knew more about Spencer than he ever wanted to.

Chad's castoff.

He left the bakery, hating himself, hating Kane's Crossing, yet hating what Chad Spencer had done to Meggie even more.

Chapter Two

Meg tried her best to stop shivering, but she couldn't.

Nick Cassidy, here again. She hadn't seen him since she was twelve, running around exploring abandoned houses with him, hiking along the length of train tracks to see where they led.

She pushed through the swinging door that led to the back of the bakery. There, she started to gather ingredients for some of her infamous chocolate cakes. Anything to keep her mind off Nick's return to Kane's Crossing.

She looked through the steam-shrouded window, catching a shape just outside.

Nick. Her gaze took a leisurely stroll over him—one she'd been too stunned to enjoy earlier.

He cast a long shadow in the dusty, autumn-leaf-strewn street, his black sunglasses barricading a gaze that seemed to be trained on the sign above her bakery's rear entrance. Under the dark brown leather jacket that matched his scuffed cowboy boots, a flannel shirt flapped in the breeze, covering broad shoulders and a wide chest. In spite of all this darkness, he had hair the color of shaded wheat—earthy, begging for a hand to skim through its bounty. The ends curled up, as if in need of a good trim.

Most acutely of all, Meg again noticed his faded blue jeans, how he wore them like a badge of apathy, obviously not concerned that the raggedy hole allowed her a taunting peek of one tanned knee. The patch of skin against the threadbare denim nudged at Meg's imagination. It was a chink in the rest of his armor— a heart-tugging flaw. She pictured herself sliding her hand into the frayed hole, running her thumb over his kneecap, skimming her fingers over the skin behind his knee.

He lowered his shaded gaze to meet hers, seemingly sensing her scrutiny. The black-ice mask of his sunglasses revealed no emotion. Meg pulled back from the window, her blood pounding so hard it crashed in her ears.

Nick backed up a step, then ambled down Main Street to disappear behind a red-and-blue Welcome Home, Chad banner that hung with a lopsided sneer between the side of the Mercantile Department Store and Darla's Beauty Shop. He moved with the purpose of a gunslinger, slow and easy, with the sleekness of a knife's edge.

Gone, from her life again, just like that.

She wondered what he wanted in a dinky one-horse town like Kane's Crossing, what he wanted with Chad Spencer. If she didn't have so much at stake here, she would've tipped her own hat to the place months ago.

Before all the trouble. Before she'd made a complete and utter disaster of her life.

Meg sighed. Men in dark clothing with an equally dark posture—the stuff of fantasy. A safe flirtation locked inside her. Grown-up Nick had been a man to strike fear into every good-girl cell of Meg's body, not that there were many of those left. She'd spent the last of her innocence five months ago and, yet, here she was, lesson unlearned, salivating over the hole in a man's jeans.

Meg mixed the ingredients into a bowl, frustration making her stir a little too zealously. And if she was miffed by Nick's return, Deacon Chaney would no doubt feel a million times worse. It was hard enough for the elderly man to live through all the slings and arrows of town without having to face the man who'd been accused of destroying his store sixteen years ago.

She was getting to be pretty good at shouldering the town's gibes, as well. But the sharp-tongued speculation about who the father of her baby might be still smarted. And it scared her to death. If anyone found out who'd fathered her unborn child, she'd lose her expected family for certain.

But Meg wouldn't let that happen.

What are you afraid of? she asked herself. Was she afraid her child would someday reject her, much like her own family had? Would she feel as much pain as she had when Aunt Valentine had died? Or would it be a dull ache, like she'd felt when the baby's father had told her she hadn't meant anything to him? That she'd be a memory once he'd left for the far corners of the world the next morning?

Chad Spencer will have no part of this child, she promised herself.

She'd die before that happened.

* * *

Two hours later Meg locked up the bakery and wrapped her sheepskin coat around her to ward off the autumn's night chill. Fire smoke puffed from chimneys just off Main Street, making the air heavy with loneliness. When she got home, nobody would be there waiting for her. After Aunt Valentine had succumbed to a heart attack five months ago, Meg had realized that she'd probably be alone for the rest of her life. But then, she'd gotten pregnant, and she knew she'd always have someone, *if* Chad didn't come back to town and claim the baby for himself.

Once again, Nick Cassidy entered her mind. What did he want with Chad?

She reached into her coat pocket, fisting the wad of twenties he'd flipped on the counter to pay for his barely touched coffee. It was enough to get her through a month or two of groceries. How did he come by so much money that he could afford to flick it around as if it were confetti?

Pride tapped her on the shoulder. She couldn't keep this so-called tip. If she saw him again, she'd have to give it back.

If she saw him again.

Her body warmed just thinking about Nick. Boy, he'd grown up good. She'd always loved being with him, climbing trees, eating snowcones as they watched stream water ripple over their shoeless feet. The summers she'd visited Kane's Crossing had been some of the best times of her life, but when Nick had come to live in town… Those had been the glory days.

He'd been gracious about allowing a pip-squeak like her to run around with him for a couple of months.

Then again, he'd been "the new boy," friendless. But they'd clicked automatically that day when Chad had been trying to lift her skirt with a stick. Nick had walked right up to him and defended her. No one else had done that before. He was her instant hero.

She'd returned the next summer, and they'd fallen into a daily groove together, experiencing everything Kane's Crossing could offer two lonely kids.

But now... Now he was so different. Edged with bitterness, his eyes almost empty with disappointment.

Her body warmed with the very thought of his eyes, the way they'd roamed over her body with the heat of a falling star. Ever since he'd left the bakery, she'd wondered what it'd feel like to have his hands follow the paths his gaze had taken, to have his hands slip under her sweater, rub her skin, push her against his hard chest.

Stop it, Meg, she thought. It was no use. She'd never even see him again. The thought left an empty place inside her. If only they could've been friends again. She was in need of someone to talk to.

She shivered and started walking past the closed boutiques and stores that lined the street, Halloween colors trimming the displays. As she passed the barbershop, she held back a wave of nausea. A picture of Chad in his high school football uniform graced the window, his slick smile adding to the image of blond perfection.

How could she have been that stupid?

She was so lost in thought that she'd all but ignored the sound of footsteps behind her. Meg clutched at her coat and purse, ready to belt whomever was trailing her.

One, two, three—

As she whipped around, purse flying, Gary Joanson jumped away from her.

"Ah! Wait, Meg!"

She stood, legs apart, ready to defend herself. "What do you want, Gary? Didn't you and your friends hurl enough insults at me this afternoon?"

He hung his head. "Sorry about that. You know how Sonny and Junior get when they've been drinking."

Yes, she knew. She'd experienced the lash of their taunts several times over. "What do you want?"

"Well, you closed up shop before I could catch you there." Shuffle. "I was just wondering if you could fix the missus one of your baby cakes?"

The urge to roll her eyes consumed her. "Gary, I've told you guys—"

"I know. But she believes all that hooey about your spells and magic. She says Valentine passed on her witch skills to you, Meg. And last time Jemma Carson ate one of your baby cakes, she got pregnant the next week. Just like Judy Henry and Sheri Duarte and…"

The list went on. Somehow the good people of Kane's Crossing had gotten it into their heads that she had a magic touch. Eat one of her blueberry pies, and you'd find a boyfriend. Eat a simple chocolate cake baked by her supernatural hands, and you'd become pregnant within the month. Kane's Crossing didn't like her much, but they sure held great respect for her eerie baking skills. And Meg took advantage of the awe. It was the only way she made money, besides the tourists.

"Okay, Gary. I'll make one tomorrow. May I go home now?"

At the mention of her "house on haunted hill," Gary's eyes bulged. Meg was the only one in town who didn't feel the need to cross herself as she walked past, what with its thunderous gables and legendary widow's walk. Even the windows looked like eyes watching the town with contempt.

"Thank you, Meg. Sure I can't walk you—" he gulped "—home?"

"I'm fine."

He scampered out of sight. Silly, henpecked man. Gary Joanson had always been a follower, never standing up to Chad's antics.

Maybe she could bake a pie and tell him it made one grow a backbone. He'd probably believe it, as would his fuss-budget wife.

A low voice startled her. "Have you been slipping mickies to this town?"

She turned around, fingers spread over her heart. "I thought you'd left."

Nick Cassidy ambled into the circle of light made by a street lamp, thumbs resting in his belt loops. Her heart beat double time, punching her chest with a voodoo cadence.

Yeah, he'd grown up good. Her gaze strayed to the hole in his jeans.

"I walked around, took another look at my old home." His eyes were eclipsed by some dark memory. "Did some more thinking."

She must've been trembling something awful, because he reached out, fingers twining around her coat collar, and he pulled the material closer together. She flinched, unsure of what his intentions were, but all he did was smile a little. It transformed his face, as if a ray of light had suffused his soul. Just as quickly, the image vanished.

She grinned, warming at his proximity. He was

watching out for her again, just as he'd done when they were kids. The thought twisted her heart around.

"What did you think about?" She almost regretted asking, wondering if the question would push him away once again.

"Everything. Mostly my reasons for coming to Kane's Crossing." He paused. "Do you walk home by yourself every night?"

"Sometimes my friend Rachel drives me. You wouldn't know her since she moved into town about two years ago." Meg laughed. "She hasn't had time to develop a fear of me yet."

They started walking, matching each other step for step, the sound of his booted feet shooting off the whitewashed buildings. It almost seemed as if he were aiming bullets into the sky, announcing his presence.

Meg reveled in his nearness, in the way she came just to above his shoulder, in the way he smelled of leather. She couldn't believe she was walking with Nick Cassidy again, but, instead of feeling like a best friend, she felt entirely different. What would he do if she wrapped an arm around his lean waist, held him to her, stood on tiptoe to bury her nose in the crook of his shoulder and neck?

She passed a hand over her belly. It'd never happen, especially after Chad's treatment of her.

He spoke first, a cloud of air trailing from his lips because of the crisp weather. "When I came back here, I didn't expect to find you. I thought you'd be back in San Diego."

Thank goodness he was talking to her again. *Really* talking. Not using monosyllabic words as he had in the bakery. She tried to smile and failed. "I can't go back there."

"Don't your parents live on the coast?"

She couldn't bring herself to talk about her parents, the pain, the agony of what she'd done to be kicked out of the house at the age of fourteen. It'd been something so horrible that she woke up with nightmares even now.

She absently touched her belly, the life within. "Yes, they do. I suppose. I've lived with Aunt Valentine since shortly after you left…" She hesitated, hoping he'd elaborate on that fateful night at Chaney's Drugstore. She wasn't really surprised when he kept his silence. Well, at least she'd tried.

"After Aunt Valentine passed on, she left everything to me. And I decided to stay here."

"I'm sorry to hear she's gone. Valentine was great."

Meg couldn't hold back a smile. "Remember how she'd invite you over for dinner and, 'Oh, by the way, would you weed my garden, Nick, dear?'"

"I was a sucker for her pot roast at any cost." Nick chuckled, sending waves of contentment through Meg's body. She stiffened, fighting the warmth, making sure she didn't give him an opportunity to hurt her.

They'd left the lights of Main Street and had turned onto the dirt road that led past the graveyard and toward Meg's home. Hovering over the stark, white tombstones, the shape of the house on the hill was visible even in the dark. It loomed with the profile of a sorcerer's hat topping a bald head. No wonder all the kids told scary stories about her and Aunt Valentine.

She saw a pale object stretching along the side of the road. When she went over to investigate, Nick grabbed her hand. The contact sent a shock wave up her arm, the zing shivering into her lower stomach.

"What're you doing?" she asked, breathless.

He let go of her, as if he'd touched a live electrical wire. "You've got to be careful, Meggie. You can't go traipsing into ditches."

"We knocked-up damsels are pretty much able to make our own decisions." She lifted her chin into the air, watching Nick from the corner of her eye. "Whether they're good or bad."

He was grinning again, for heaven's sake. She hadn't been sure she could get another one out of him.

He used the advantage of his long legs to move ahead of her, and she stood back, as he lifted the object.

Clouds uncovered the moon as he spread it wide. "We miss you, Chad" was painted in red and blue lettering. One of those darn banners the ladies' auxiliary had been hanging all over town. She wondered if the wind had blown this particular sign away from Main Street, or if someone felt as strongly about Chad as she did, tearing down the banner and tossing it into what Nick would've called a "ditch."

Nick stared at it a moment, then crumpled it to the ground, stepping on it as he clutched her hand again. His grip almost smashed her finger bones.

"That hurts," she said, keeping her voice as level as possible.

He glanced at her hand, lifted it, and ran his fingers over hers. Meg almost melted to the dirt with a rush of liquid heat.

"Sorry," he said, his voice purring down her skin. Then, he patted her hand as if she were a five-year-old. They started walking again.

"Why are those signs all over town?" he asked.

She sighed heavily. Chad again. "Chad went to Europe in order to learn part of the family trade. A branch of the illustrious Spencer family runs several banks over there, and he's learning from the best. I guess they want to expand the bank business once he returns to the States.'' There. She'd said it without tripping over her words, without letting on that Chad had ripped out her heart.

Nick seemed to know anyway. He stopped their progress, taking her shoulders into his hands, watching her carefully, his mouth set in a line. He seemed like a shadow, so tall, mysterious, intimidating. She swallowed, the sound much too obvious over his silence.

He ran his index finger under her chin, cuffing it playfully. Meg wanted to grab him right there and then, giving in to the promise of her afternoon fantasy. Darn pregnancy hormones.

He said, ''I have a bad feeling that King of the World hurt you, Meggie.''

Moonlight. His low, pint-of-whiskey voice. His shadow lingering over her. It was all enough to make her want to run away because he'd changed so much. Changed into something she couldn't ever hope to have in her life.

''No, you're wrong,'' she said, hoping she sounded as airy as she had when she used to dress like a rock-and-roll Gypsy girl.

He settled his hands on her upper arms, cupping them, leaving her weak. She could tell by the tone of his voice that he'd gone on to a more serious subject. ''I don't live here, so trust me. Spencer's the father. Am I wrong?''

''Yes. I mean, yes, you're wrong,'' she lied.

She hadn't fooled him, judging by his hangdog look of disappointment. ''I knew it.''

He knew. All the work she'd gone through to hide it, and he'd guessed her secret right off the bat. She'd never confirmed the rumors in town about her baby. For all the people of Kane's Crossing knew, she'd gotten pregnant when she'd gone upstate to settle Aunt Valentine's estate five months ago. But she knew better. Obviously Nick knew better, too.

A black look crossed over his face, and her heart seemed to stop from the intensity of it. He took a couple of steps back, away from her.

"Don't look so sad. We're going to make things right."

She shook her head. "No one can know the truth, Nick. When Chad comes back to town, I'm afraid he'll want my baby." She choked, thinking about what she'd done to get kicked out of her parents' house. If Chad were to discover her ineptitude, he'd pounce all over her, maybe even drag her through a custody battle. She'd lose her baby for certain.

"He'd never marry me—the witch who lives on haunted hill. What if he took my baby, and I never saw my child again? You know he can do it. His family has so much money and power..."

"Get out of town."

"And where would I go? Not back to San Diego, to my parents, you can be sure of that. I've got nowhere, Nick. Everything I own is here."

"Sell the house."

If only she could. "That place has been in my family since eighteen sixty-two. I promised Aunt Valentine before she died that I'd never sell it." She laughed. "I'm between a rock and a hard place. Do you understand?"

Nick ran a hand through his hair. Was he nervous about something?

"Nick?"

He cleared his throat, looking so lost in the middle of a town that hated him. The sight made her want to hold him and never let go.

"Meggie, you can give your child a name. It's the only solution."

There was no solution as far as she was concerned. "Thanks for the optimism, but I have no idea what to do."

He took a deep breath. "You can marry me."

Chapter Three

Meggie looked as if a slight wind could've knocked her over.

"Did you say something about marrying you?"

Nick couldn't believe he'd said it himself, but it made sense. He'd come to Kane's Crossing to dish out revenge and, at the same time, right some wrongs. This was a perfect way to start. "Wouldn't it help, Meggie? You said yourself that you're afraid Chad will take the baby from you. How could he do that if we're married?"

"Because you're not the father." She turned away from him, tucking her hands into her coat pockets.

Moonlight gleamed over her curly hair. He wondered how she'd react if he ran his hands through it, but he nixed the idea. Nick had never been one to lose his heart to a woman; as a matter of fact, he'd spent his life insulating himself from love. As with the string of foster homes he'd left in his wake, he'd never allowed himself to settle down with one person. He couldn't believe he was about to do it now.

He corrected himself. It wasn't as if he was going to pledge his heart to Meggie. This marriage would be more like a business arrangement, a protective gesture to keep Meggie and her child safe from Spencer's games. The King of Kane's Crossing had already shaded his summer friend's eyes with sadness. Nick wouldn't allow him to do any more damage. Not if he could help it.

He aimed his words at her back. "Who in this town knows that I'm not the father? You've made it a point to keep his identity a secret."

"What's in it for you, Nick?"

He watched her back, her red hair cascading over the enormous coat that swallowed her whole. She was so small, so alone. Nick hadn't found many bright moments lately in his life, but now he actually felt a glimmer of hope. Maybe he could be useful to Meggie. Maybe he could matter.

But she was right. What was in it for him? His dark soul had a ready answer. Revenge and justice, music to his ears.

He'd come to Kane's Crossing equipped with a Machiavellian plan, something that would ruin Chad Spencer financially. Anger had driven Nick Cassidy to earn his millions—anger and the need to rise above what everyone predicted he'd be. A failure. A good-for-nothing who went around bombing buildings.

Nick had earned his way through college, penny by penny, until he'd joined forces with a friend whose family was in the banking field. They'd given Nick his start, preparing him for the day when he'd gathered enough money through solid investments to buy his first business. He'd sold it to another owner for far more than he could've imagined it was worth. He'd done it again…and again, until he'd collected a mind-blowing sum of money.

Then, a few months ago, when he'd found himself thrown from a car—just this short of death—he'd decided to return to Kane's Crossing. His money and business experience fueling his desire to take away Spencer's power, the time was now right for some payback.

His plan was simple. His old college friend—who'd long since earned a corporate-raider-tough reputation—would buy up Spencer's businesses, one by one, for Nick. The toy factory, the market, the hardware store, the big department store… And, finally, the banks. His college buddy would engineer a hostile takeover, giving the Spencers no room to expand their business empire. Maybe he'd leave them their dog-grooming shop, just to allow for a little mercy. By then, Spencer would've learned his lesson.

Someday he would know that Nick Cassidy had taken away Chad's power as easily as Chad had taken away Nick's family.

Nick had almost scrapped his plan, wondering if he was being too harsh. But as he'd driven his battered pickup around town today, after visiting Meggie at her bakery, he'd noticed that most of the poorer families he'd known from his youth had moved away. He'd stopped on the outskirts of the county to chat up some old men who decorated the front porch of a general store. What had happened to the families? he'd asked.

The old men had had no idea who he was because Nick had pretended to be searching for old friends.

They'd given him information without a second thought. The families had owed Chad Spencer money, and, not being able to pay off their loans, Spencer had foreclosed on their properties. The news had sparked Nick's temper even more than before. Spencer was truly ruthless, feeding on the less fortunate like a dog gnawing on bones.

What if Nick could give these families their property again?

He now had more to fight for than just his own disappointments. He'd find justice for the displaced families, as well.

And Meggie was one of Spencer's victims. He'd fight for her, too.

She'd turned around, her eyes running over him with a suspicious burn. How the hell had Spencer even gotten his hands on her? Damn, it was too painful to even think about.

She held out her hand. A bundle of money spilled through her fingers. His tip from this afternoon.

"You don't owe me anything," she said.

Yes, he did. He owed her the world on a chain for the happiness she'd loaned him for a short time during one sun-dappled, near-perfect summer.

"Keep it, Meggie."

Her chin raised a little. "I don't accept pity money, or pity proposals."

That was his Meggie. When he'd first seen her in the bakery, he'd thought she'd lost her fire. But it was back, with a vengeance.

He nodded toward the fistful of cash. "Imagine how well I could provide for your son or daughter."

"Nick—"

"We could set up a trust fund for the baby. He or she would never lack for anything."

She stopped talking, cocked her head.

"We could even keep Valentine's home in trust, have someone else take care of it. You could leave this place with no thoughts of how you'll make a living."

"How did you get all this money?"

He didn't like the expression on her face. Accusatory. Suddenly he felt fourteen again, with cuffs around his wrists, the sheriff breathing down his neck, yelling at him, pointing a stubby finger at the charred remains of Chaney's Drugstore.

He wouldn't have bothered to defend himself to anyone else but Meggie. His voice was a harsh whisper, edged by shame. "It was all legal."

She shook her head, thrusting out her cash-laden fist once again. "That's not what I meant." Meggie's glance combed the grass. "I know nothing about you, Nick. I'd be marrying a stranger."

"I'm the same guy I always was."

"No." Her hand fell to her side. "You're not."

He knew it was true. Years of darkness had shadowed his brow, had given him a more predatory walk. He'd never possess the optimistic swagger of a teenager. Never again.

Why did she have to be so sad? Everyone changed. You just had to use your experiences to your own advantage. Didn't she realize he just wanted to help her?

He walked nearer to Meggie, his fingers itching to tilt up her chin until her gaze met his. He'd never ached to touch a woman so much in his life.

"Nobody's the same as they were sixteen years ago. But I haven't changed that much." He still carried a bright torch of anger. That would never change, not until Chad Spencer got his due.

As if sensing the intensity of his desires, she stepped away from him. "I still don't understand why you'd want to raise a child who's not even yours. The child of a man you hate."

Guilt struck him a blow. What could he say to her? *Meggie, I want the man who ruined my chances for a normal family life to suffer, knowing that I have control of his ultimate possession—his child?*

How would she react, knowing that some dark part of his heart beat—no, *survived*—with thoughts of revenge?

"Trust me to do the right thing," he said, ignoring all the doubts in his mind. Yeah, trust him to use her in his crusade against the town golden boy.

Meggie was silent a moment. Nick took the opportunity to enjoy how the moon's milky sheen smoothed her skin. He wondered if the curve of her belly would look so soft. What would it feel like to cup his hands over her stomach? To run his fingers over the life pulsing just beneath?

Maybe he wouldn't even be around to know. From the way Meggie was reacting to his proposal, he was in for a long walk home.

He couldn't stand the pressure she was under. "Listen," he said, "you don't have to decide right now. You can contact me at the Edgewater Motel off the highway, okay?"

"I don't know what to say."

He tried to smile. "Worry about it later."

"Take your money." She held out her hand one more time.

"No."

Her eyes widened. Nick recalled that Aunt Valentine rarely told her favorite niece no; obviously, she hadn't expected him to say it, either.

She shrugged, seeming embarrassed. She opened her mouth, probably to slam him with a smart remark, but she was interrupted by the dry swish of tires burning rubber over the gravel road.

A mint Mustang convertible seemed to fly out of the moon's center as it sped toward them. Long hair and slender arms sprouted from the seats as a carload of females roared down the road.

"What the hell?"

Meggie turned her back on them. "Don't even look at them, Nick," she yelled over the "Whoo!" of celebratory voices.

The car screeched to a halt next to them. Seven girls, all smooshed into the confines of a sports vehicle. He'd never understand the female species.

The driver had sparkling eyes and a short, pixie haircut. "Hey, Meg, want a ride?"

He didn't know whether or not the question was mocking, but before he could decide, a passenger chimed in.

"Yeah, Witchy Poo, join us." She turned to the other girls. "Maybe she can make our car fly over the moon!"

Nick was about to step up for Meggie when the driver whirled on her friends.

"Pipe down, you harpies." She looked at Nick, then at Meggie, who wasn't even facing the car. "You okay, Meg?"

Nick was close enough to see Meggie's jaw clench. After a moment she said, "I'm fine."

"Go!" screamed one of the harpies. The driver

looked at Meggie once more, at Nick, then let out a deafening yell of joy before laying pedal to the metal and taking off in a spray of dirt. The car roared down the road, past the spindly black-iron angels of the cemetery gates, past rickety horse-pasture fences. Voices faded into the chilly, autumn-swept air, tree leaves rustling in the aftermath.

Meggie watched them leave. "You wanted Chad Spencer? Well, that's the closest you're going to get."

"What do you mean?"

Meggie's smile didn't reach her eyes. "The driver was Ashlyn, Chad's sister."

Nick clenched his hands into fists, trying hard to ignore the fire in his heart. "What're they doing tearing up the roads like that?"

Meggie looked past him, toward the graveyard's angel gate. Nick thought about Aunt Valentine, and where she might be buried.

"That was Ashlyn's plan for a friend's bachelorette party. Raising Cain around town, flying a few bras on flag poles, posting a few anti-Spencer posters in windows. Anything to salute her brother's superiority. She does her best to embarrass the family." Meggie turned to Nick, her eyes suddenly brimming with tears.

A breeze whistled past them, humming a low, mournful tune in his ear. He had to hold himself back from smoothing a strand of bobbing hair from the corner of her soft, red mouth. So vulnerable. He wanted to protect her from all the hurt in the world.

She half laughed. "I think she despises Chad as much as you do. She's had to live up to his perfection all these years. I almost like her."

How could she feel that way about anything Spencer? He couldn't understand. "A bachelorette party?"

he asked, wanting to steer the subject away from Ashlyn's brother.

"I baked the bride-to-be an angel food cake my own supernatural self. I should know."

He laughed, actually laughed, at that. She did, too. He was glad they could agree on something, even if it did border on the obscene. This time he didn't stop himself from touching her, sketching a thumb down her cheek. Soft, so soft. "I'll walk you to your door."

She'd frozen under his touch. As she looked into his eyes, he saw fear, trepidation. Maybe some memories she'd rather forget. "I'll manage."

With that Meggie pulled away from him and climbed the steps up the hill to the massive black door of her home. Dark spiderwebby decorations surrounded the door frame like sentinels. He watched until she disappeared.

She held the rest of their lives in her hands. He hoped she'd make the right decision.

Three days later Meg still hadn't come to a definite decision.

"Now, don't do anything hasty, Meg," said Rachel Shane as she drove both of them to the Edgewater Motel. Her rattrap of a car bounced over the county roads, causing Rachel to slow down and Meg to cradle her belly.

Meg shot her best friend a have-faith-in-me glance. "Am I the flighty type? I've thought long and hard about this."

"A stranger. The guy could be from Mars for all you know."

"I'm pretty secure in the belief that he's earthbound, Rachel." She understood her friend's concerns. Not only did they echo her own, but Rachel had her own issues that shed a wary light on Meg's situation.

At the beginning of the year Rachel's husband had disappeared, leaving his wife and five-year-old daughter behind on their bluegrass-rich horse farm. Rachel wasn't a Kane's Crossing native, so she'd been experiencing much the same troubles from the town as Meg. They were united in their loneliness, outsiders who'd allowed skeletons to creep out of their closets.

Rachel's gray-green eyes searched Meg's. "I think you're not telling me everything."

What? That Nick Cassidy had held her in thrall since she'd seen him standing in her bakery like a lone cowboy waiting for a gunfight? That he made her think thoughts best left sleeping? Not even Rachel would understand Meg's attraction to this man. She was still railing against men in general—Chad, and her husband, Matthew, in particular.

Rachel continued. "Your dignity was thoroughly trounced by Chad five short months ago, so I don't understand why you're so hot to marry anyone. Besides, you should listen to a girl with experience, one who knows about men who leave home to never return. I hope you're thinking twice—no, three, four times—about this marriage proposal. It's nuts."

Pride had almost convinced Meg to turn down Nick's suggestion right on the spot, but then Ashlyn Spencer and her party had driven by, reminding Meg of how much she didn't really belong in Kane's Crossing. The insults would never stop. Neither would the moral censure for having a baby out of wedlock.

She'd thought a little harder about Nick's proposal. She knew it wasn't a love match and, even so, the thought of the security he offered her and her unborn child was tempting. That's why she needed to talk with him again, just to decide once and for all how she was going to handle a child on a single gal's budget.

They drove past the autumn-laced trees that lurked over the highway, slowing once they saw the rickety, neon-buzzed sign perpetually proclaiming Edgewater Motel—Vacancy. A one-story building squatted on the roadside, lined by a droopy porch complete with slouching chairs. Pink doors dotted the white-boarded walls. Meg guessed Nick was staying in room six because it was the only one with a vehicle in front of it. A lone-wolf-looking pickup truck.

Once again, she wondered how Nick had gotten rich enough to flip her a three-hundred-dollar coffee tip.

"This is it," she said, gathering her purse.

Rachel laid a hand on Meg's arm. "I'll go in with you."

Meg surveyed her friend's hospital scrubs. "The emergency room is expecting you. I can handle this. Really."

"You thought you had this Chad thing handled, too."

Meg tried to still her anxiety. "Rachel, thank you for the concern and the help. And thank you for knowing when to stop nagging me."

Most of all, she added silently, thank you for keeping my secret.

Rachel—and now Nick—had been the only two people she'd trusted. Was she about to make a mistake by putting her faith in Nick?

Rachel smiled at her, a comforting balm to Meg's nerves.

"Call if you need anything. You have my beeper number."

Meg got out of the car. "You bet. And, Rachel?"

Her friend waited expectantly, a worried frown on her face.

"I hope you hear something about Matthew. Good luck."

Rachel's eyes held a painful collage colored in grays. "Well, I'm not paying that detective to sit around. I'd better hear something about my vaporous husband soon." She waved. "I'll watch you for a minute."

Meg shut the car door. Through the open window, she said, "Why does everyone worry about us pregnant gals? I'm not going to explode within the next minute."

Rachel cocked an eyebrow, tapping her nails on the steering wheel.

Meg took a deep breath, then marched up the stairs to number six. She lifted her chin and knocked, resisting the temptation to peek at Rachel.

The door opened to showcase Nick, ruggedly handsome in a T-shirt that hugged every dip and curve of his wide chest, every ridged stomach muscle. The white material tucked into his faded jeans, a different pair, this one with a hole on the side of the upper thigh. It was almost as if he'd predicted her fascination with the chinks in his armor.

She realized she'd been gawking at him only when she heard Rachel's clunky car wheeze away. Nick grinned down at her, resting his arm up against the door frame. Something wicked urged her to nestle a palm against his cut waist, slide it upward, over his stomach, the side of his chest, until she could dig her fingers in the tender spot under his arm.

Bad girl. Dumb girl. Girl who had no business even

thinking about sex stuff after Chad had proven how incapable she was of handling an intimate situation.

And Nick wasn't helping, with his insolent smile and leathery scent. He was so close she could hear him breathing. She wasn't happy to find that she'd been matching him, breath for breath.

"Hi," he said softly, still leaning.

"Hello. May I come in?" Or maybe not. Could be an awful idea here.

He paused a moment, his pale blue eyes running over her body until she blushed inside and out. What could a man like him see in a getting-fatter-by-the-moment, bad-news girl? He grinned again, backing up to allow her entrance.

She stepped into the room, thinking she was doing pretty well poise-wise until she saw it.

The bed.

She'd just stepped into a situation she might not be able to handle.

Chapter Four

Nick rested his hands on his lean hips, obviously amused with Meg's motel-bed shock. "It's not going to swallow you up."

But it sure consumed the room, thought Meg. It was king-size, robed with a quilted gingham pattern. The Bates Motel furnishings gave Meg a shiver: two Spartan nightstands, a dreary lamp, a tiny TV that required you to switch channels by hand dial and a dresser capped by a long, bleary mirror... And, wouldn't you know, the mirror reflected the entire length of the bed. She didn't even turn around to look at the shower for fear of fainting right on the spot.

"Of course it won't swallow me." She cleared her throat as she turned her back on said furniture. She tried to laugh off the nervousness, but what came out of her lungs was far more terrifying than the room. A near cackle. A genuine, Witchy Poo, yikes-I'm-being-chased-by-the-devil cry for help. She clamped her lips together before subjecting them both to more terror.

Now that she'd gotten both Nick and the bed out of the same line of sight, she felt more comfortable. "You're probably wondering why I'm here."

Silence. No need for words. Nick merely crossed his muscled arms over his chest and rested his back against the wall.

She took a deep breath and exhaled. "The truth of it is, I'm still not sure what to tell you about marriage."

He nodded. A muscle flexed in one of his arms, a quick, jerky motion, almost as if he'd blocked an incoming fist to the gut.

Could this man be a father to her child? Could he forget that Chad Spencer had taken a pretty active part in creating him or her? Meg held back another nervous laugh. It didn't get tenser than this. "I've thought of so many reasons not to say yes to you."

"I heard them the other night," he said, his voice low, as skin-tingling as fingernails lightly scratching down her back.

She thought of how nice it'd be to have someone like Nick around every night, someone who actually warmed her heart, her body. Somebody who—maybe someday—could care about her. Aunt Valentine would never come back again. Her parents would never welcome her into their arms. All bets were off on Chad becoming a part of her family. Meg had no doubt Nick cared, but would he be a real family to her?

Then again, how many men wanted to marry a woman who was about to give birth to an illegitimate child? Maybe Nick was the closest she'd ever get to having a family again. Even if, every time she peeked over at him leaning against the wall, she saw the reflection of foster home abandonment in the way he crossed his arms, the way he kept his silence.

What secrets did this man hide from her? Did she really want to know?

All she was certain of was that she'd always have secrets of her own. Especially the one about her family and why they'd never, ever, allow her into their home again. It was a secret that, if revealed, could turn Nick against her. One that could give Chad supreme power if he decided to engage her in a custody battle for her baby.

This marriage could even the playing field with Chad. And that was it, the answer she'd been searching for. It was too bad she couldn't enter this marriage because of love, but love was a luxury she couldn't afford after all the mistakes she'd made with her life.

Somewhere in her brain, Chad was laughing at her. It was the same laugh she'd heard the night after they'd made love—or whatever it was called. It'd certainly had nothing to do with love. Fear had driven her, fear of being alone for the rest of her life.

Nick's gravely voice shoved Chad's laughter out of her perception. "Have I lost you, Meggie?"

Her heart jumped, then she smiled. He was referring to her woolgathering, nothing else. If she turned down his proposal, it wouldn't tear him apart. Nick had no emotional stake in this.

"You haven't lost me." Not yet. "I still don't understand why you'd offer to do this. I guess I need to know before this goes any further."

His arms remained crossed. "You're right, I haven't explained anything." He shook his head. "I don't know what I was expecting you to say when you don't realize where I'm coming from."

He motioned toward the bed, a grin hiding in his eyes. "It's the only seat in the house, Meggie, and I know it can't be comfortable standing on your feet for too long."

She reluctantly edged onto the bed, sighing as the weight was taken off her legs. Maybe Nick would be a good husband—thoughtful, fantasy-inducing... She wiped her mind clean of wicked thoughts and waited for him to explain.

"I guess I should make it clear that our marriage would be in name only. That should soothe your thoughts a little."

Something in her heart took a dive. "But—marriage?"

"Yeah, I know it's a big step." He looked her straight in the eyes, a soul-searing request for faith. "I wasn't the one who set off the bomb in Chaney's Drugstore, and I mean to correct the misconception."

Meg felt her eyebrows pulling together. He was kidding, right? "Nick, the bombing happened sixteen years ago. You're still obsessing over it?"

Wrong thing to say. He stood a little taller, stiffer, his arms tightening over his broad chest, his strong shoulders lifting as if counteracting another burden that had been hefted onto them. "The Reno family was the closest thing I ever had to a normal life. It's something worth fighting for. When Spencer set off that bomb, he didn't just destroy a building, he blew up their confidence in me. My parents never talked to me again. Same with my brother, Sam."

Meg hadn't realized the depth of his hatred until now. She wondered anew why he wanted to be a father to Chad's child.

Nick continued. "I can't get my parents back. And

Sam might not even want to look me in the eye again. But I'm sure as hell going to make sure Chad Spencer never hurts anyone in this town, and that includes you, Meggie. You and your baby.''

Her throat burned from emotion. It'd been a long time since someone had cared this much about her. Aunt Valentine would've gone out on a limb for Meg, and now Nick was here to take her place. She could actually have a family again.

The only drawback was this raging anger that emanated from Nick's every word. It frightened her, yet his knight-in-shining-armor attitude all but overshadowed that fear. His gesture of marriage touched her, made her feel like a person again. It had been ages since she'd felt like more than a whipping boy for the Kane's Crossing's gossip committee, even if she did deserve every harsh word as punishment for what she'd done in San Diego all those years ago.

Yet, she couldn't help thinking that it was this same sort of anger that had driven her parents to kick her out of her home, the same anger that had basically orphaned her, cut off any hope of ever seeing her parents again. If she were to marry Nick, she'd have to live with anger. Could she do it?

She raised her gaze to his. What she saw startled her. A flash of pale lightning in his blue eyes, zinging her, making her go weak. His desire to protect her baby was a gift she couldn't turn down.

Yes, she could do it.

She tried to smile. "How soon can we make arrangements?"

His shoulders relaxed slightly, but nothing else changed. Meg tried not to let that be a bad omen.

"I'll make an appointment with the county clerk today. Remember—'' he moved away from the wall to stand in front of her, to rest his hand on her shoulder as a best friend would ''—you've got no worries now. I'll take care of Spencer.''

Meg wished this were true, but she knew she'd exchanged one set of worries for another. Her new concerns had more to do with holes in faded jeans and eyes the shade of wishes gone by.

Days later, Nick adjusted his necktie for the last time. He hated wearing these things because it felt like—what else?—a noose. Even more so today, his wedding day.

He looked around the small, flower-laden room of the county courthouse, wishing he and Meggie could just get a certificate and be done with the whole process. But, in spite of his discomfort, he knew that Meggie would want some sort of special touch. A woman wasn't a bride every day, so he'd arranged for the county clerk to marry them in a civil ceremony.

So, here he was, waiting for Deacon Chaney, of all people, to walk his blushing bride down the narrow aisle. Nick was a great fan of irony, so he could appreciate having Chaney, the man whose building he'd been accused of bombing, on hand to give away Meggie. But the second witness Meggie had selected at the last moment was too much.

Ashlyn Spencer stood beside him, bouncing up and down in time to the recorded harp-music wedding march. A Spencer, at his own wedding. Life didn't get more hilarious than this.

He'd watched Meggie with admiration as she'd calmly handled every stumbling block. First, Rachel Shane, Meggie's best friend, had been called to the county hospital on an emergency, leaving them without a witness to their nuptials. Always the quick thinker, Meggie had hijacked Deacon Chaney, her lone customer, before closing the bakery early. Then, as Nick had driven past the general store on the edge of town, Meggie had realized that a second witness would be to their advantage.

Ashlyn had been rocking in a dilapidated porch swing, smoking a cigar with the old men, cracking jokes and generally acting un-Spencer-like. With a gleam in her eye, Meggie had hopped out of the pickup, growing belly and all, and escorted Ashlyn to join Deacon in the back of the vehicle.

In spite of the wedding party, Nick had a feeling that his life was about to change for the better.

Meggie appeared, with Deacon hanging off her arm as a dazed father figure. Nick's heart clenched when he saw her flushed skin, her genuine smile. She carried a modest bouquet of yellow-and-purple wildflowers that Ashlyn had gathered while they'd waited for the couples ahead of them to tie the knot. Some of the star-shaped petals had made it to her hair, lingering in the red curls, making her look like a flower child from the sixties. Even her clothes were slightly off kilter, reminiscent of the Gypsy girl she used to resemble. She wore a long-sleeved, shimmery, soft-pink dress that bagged at the waist and fell in a rainfall of material to her ankles. The texture reminded him of a dragonfly's wings—luminous, catching the glow of her skin like the blush of a sunrise. A pearl choker encircled her neck, so Nick suddenly didn't feel so persecuted at having to wear a tie.

He'd decided to dress for the occasion, as well, having traveled out of the county to avoid shopping at the

Spencers' stores in Kane's Crossing. He hadn't dressed to the nines—not even when he was in a casket would he ever let anyone bind him in a suit—but he seemed a decent enough groom with his creased, blue Docker-style pants and white button-down shirt. With the damned tie, of course.

As the wedding march ended, Deacon deposited Meggie at Nick's side. Then the ceremony was just a blur of diamond rings, dragonfly wings, flowers, I-dos and Meggie's soft lips. He'd shaved today, closely, thoroughly, knowing that the symbolic sealing of their union was inevitable. He'd even been looking forward to feeling Meggie's lips beneath his; he'd always wondered how soft they'd be in their rose-red fullness. However, this would be a chaste kiss, a veritable handshake to close their casual deal.

When the clerk gave them permission to kiss, they looked at each other a little warily, probably wondering where to go from here. They hadn't discussed kissing.

Hell, he hadn't even poured his entire heart out to her in that motel room, just selective pieces designed to convince her to say yes to his plan, to allow him to protect her from Spencer's cruel reach.

Deacon coughed. Ashlyn started to whistle "Colonel Bogey's March." Well, they couldn't just sit here all day.

Meggie had lowered her eyes, her cheeks reddening until they almost matched her fiery hair. Traces of freckles just about disappeared under her embarrassment. He didn't want her to think she wasn't desirable. Hell, that was far from the truth. But he also didn't want her to think he was going to be kissing her every night for the rest of her life. That would be misleading and deadly for his future. Nick Cassidy didn't do commitment—only pseudo-commitment, like this marriage.

Aw, hell. Nick lowered his head, intending to brush his mouth across hers, to just taste what he couldn't have. She must've had the same idea. As he swooped down, she swooped up. They met in the middle, their lips fitting together like a palm grooving into the small of a back. Perfectly.

Heat, strawberries and honey. That's what Meggie was made of. Even her skin was warm with the spice of her. Nick wanted to slide his hands around her back, pressing her into him, feeling the roundness of her belly—their future—curving into him, but he kept his composure.

When she started to pull away, he almost allowed it. Almost. He reached out, cupping a hand on the back of her head, entangling his fingers in ribbony hair and petals. He pressed his lips for a last taste, then slowly pulled back, brushing his mouth over hers to end it.

They looked into each other's eyes. Hers were glassy, with a star burst of fright in their green depths. He didn't dare think about his expression. Instead, he clenched his jaw, ignoring the throbbing of his mouth, his heart, his nether regions. Thank God for baggy pants.

They turned back to the county clerk, who pronounced them married. Nick looked down, feeling something in his hand. A whole purple flower, still warm, making his skin tingle.

Hell, since when did he do things as ludicrous as tingling?

As they left the room, Nick immediately whipped off his necktie. Deacon yawned, shot Nick a withering glance and strolled out of the building without another word. Nick tried to not care. The older man would find out soon enough that Chad Spencer was the one who'd taken his livelihood.

Ashlyn hugged Meggie, but didn't dare touch Nick. She stood a few feet away, an unreadable grin on her pixie face. "Congratulations, you two."

"We're glad you could be a witness," said Meggie, fanning herself. She seemed a little redder than usual.

Nick led her to the waiting area to sit. When she realized his intention, she waved him off.

Ashlyn followed them, stopping momentarily to pluck some sort of large pink-and-white flower from a county arrangement. She stuck the stem down the cleavage created by her clingy, low-necked blouse.

Nick noticed something pass through Meggie's eyes. It could have been wistfulness, as fragile as a lily pad floating over a deep green pond. Once upon a time, she'd been just as free-spirited as Ashlyn was now. Nick missed the Gypsy in her, as well.

"Well, hey," said Ashlyn, "I've got some stuff to do today, things like tearing down some banners and painting a few mustaches on portraits. Care to join me?"

Nick remembered the We Miss You, Chad banner in the ditch. Ashlyn's handiwork? He liked her more already. Not much more though.

He remained silent, the best policy.

Meggie glanced at him, as if reading his mind about Spencer. "No, thanks. Nick's moving in today."

Now was the time for talking. "Yeah," he said, folding an arm around Meggie's back, his other hand resting against her belly. Damn, it felt good, round, comfortable. The feelings stunned him, made him remove his hand and shove it into a pants' pocket. "I haven't really seen Meggie since Mead County, when she was dealing with Aunt Valentine's estate about five months ago.''

There. Let that plant a seed. Hopefully Ashlyn would spread the word that, months ago, Meggie had spent the night with him, and they'd made a baby. Red herrings could be very helpful, especially if it kept Ashlyn Spencer's brother off the right scent.

Obviously Ashlyn was an intelligent young woman. From the calculating look on her face, she'd already done the math.

Meggie spoke up. ''Let's get back to town, okay?''

And they did, silently, Ashlyn spreading her arms in the truck's flatbed breeze while both of them sat in the cab, probably wondering what they'd done. Not that Nick was having second thoughts—he just couldn't believe he was married. *Married.* Him.

But he was sitting next to the most beautiful woman in the world, with her shy smile, fourteen-carat-gold wedding ring and blossoming belly.

God, he was nervous.

Later, after dropping Ashlyn off at the general store, Nick and Meggie stood in front of her—their—house. It'd been too many years since he'd enjoyed this view. The structure resembled a sharp-eyed raven perched over Kane's Crossing. He remembered a time when the Spencer family had attempted to condemn the building, to tear it down. Maybe he loved the place so much because they hated it.

The whispering wind accompanied them up the stairs. Meggie unlocked the door.

''Wait,'' he said, tossing his full duffel bag inside to clear his arms. ''We've got a tradition to uphold here.''

"You're not going to carry me over the threshold," she said, looking at him beneath a lowered brow.

She must've thought he was crazy. "I thought maybe I would."

"Do you realize I weigh approximately as much as a beached whale? No, wait. That's just one of my thighs. You're going to break your back if you try this."

He chuckled, feeling happy. Feeling married, for God's sake. "Meggie, I've had to carry much bigger things for a long time now. Trust me."

She laughed, not the slightly demented, off-her-rocker laugh he'd heard in the motel room, but a pure sound, like water crystalling over rocks in a stream.

"Be my guest, Tarzan."

Nick undid another button on his shirt and unbuttoned his sleeves, rolling them over his forearms. He watched as Meggie's eyes followed the material. She blushed, tucking a strand of hair behind her ear.

"Ready?"

She squeezed her eyes shut, and Nick scooped her into his arms. The strawberry-tart aroma of her hair tickled his nose. "You were modest," he said. "You don't weigh any more than a baby whale."

"Thanks," she said dryly, her hand resting on his collarbone.

The touch burned, left a pulsing scar as she jerked her hand away. Maybe she felt it, too. Maybe this hadn't been such a great idea.

He stepped over the threshold, feeling immediately as if the house was welcoming him back. Memories rushed over to greet him like a home full of giggling children. Through a massive back window he could see Aunt Valentine's flower-burst garden, which Meggie had obviously kept alive. He'd weeded this garden weekly, just for the pleasure of eating Valentine's pot roast, basking in her magnolia-grandma scent and hearing her melodic voice assuring him that he'd own the world someday.

Well, here he was, owning a nice chunk of the state, at least. And he had his arms full of Valentine's niece. He wondered if the old woman would've approved.

A magnolia cloud misted over them like a shower of rice to congratulate the bride and groom. Nick's steps slowed.

Meggie watched him, gauging his reaction.

He walked over to an ancient mahogany, green-velvet-upholstered couch and laid Meggie down with the best of care, allowing his hands to linger on her ankles after resting her feet on the matching ottoman.

Meggie cleared her throat. "Am I crazy for thinking that Aunt Valentine would've approved? Even if this isn't absolutely real?"

He took in the dark, oak-etched walls, the gilded frames of ancestral pictures, the grand staircase, the heavy, ornate furniture. There was even a decadent organ in the next room, its brass pipes stretching to the high ceiling.

"This is as real as it gets, Meggie."

For the first time in sixteen years, he felt as if he'd finally come home.

It was their honeymoon night, and Meg couldn't sleep. She rolled over in her huge, canopied four-poster, watching the moonlight stream through the netting above her. Surely on a girl's honeymoon she could at least get a kiss from her new husband. Was that too much to ask?

She shut her eyes, remembering the warm press of Nick's lips as they'd closed over hers at this afternoon's ceremony. Every muddled, messed-up frame of her life had disappeared, erased, cleansed, as if all her mistakes had been washed over by the touch of him.

Had she only imagined that he wanted the embrace to last longer?

Probably. After a fairly silent dinner and lemonade on the porch, Nick had carried her up to her room, showing little interest in kissing her again. Earlier, he'd camped his duffel bag—his only belongings—in a room down the hall from hers. After gently depositing her on the bed, he'd gone to that room. No kiss, no nothing.

It was for the best, really. Her heart couldn't take another bruising like the one Chad had given her. Nick was being a gentleman.

A muffled creak sounded outside her room.

This was an old house, so she heard a lot of weird noises. They'd become a part of her life. She hadn't heard one like this before.

Creak.

Someone with bulk to their body. Someone who'd stopped outside her room.

She knew it was Nick. Holding her breath, she wondered what he was doing, thinking. Did he want to come inside? Her body wanted him to turn the wobbly crystal knob on her door to enter. Her heart blocked the possibility.

Maybe he heard her heart. She sure did, since it thundered in her ears, through her body. Another creak sounded, then another, until they grew fainter and finally stopped at the end of the hall at Nick's room.

A honeymoon without a honey.

Meg burrowed under her quilt, almost wishing Nick was there to chase away the ghosts.

Chapter Five

The next afternoon, a pre-Halloween chill crisped the air as the last customer of the day left Meg's bakery. Well, almost the last customer.

Gary Joanson leaned on the counter, his chocolate éclair untouched. "I can't believe you went and got yourself married. Say, Meg, is it true what they're whispering?" His shoulders hunched as he lowered his voice. "That Nick Cassidy's back to cause more trouble?"

Meg's heart hippity-hopped as she saw Nick opening the door. He was back to dressing in his holey jeans, flannel shirts and leather jacket. Plus the sunglasses. For a second, he seemed a lot like the stranger who'd stepped into her life mere days ago. Heck, he was still a stranger to her.

The bells jangled, making Gary sit up straighter in his chair.

Meg grinned. "Why don't you ask him yourself?"

"Never mind," mumbled Gary.

Nick slipped off his glasses, shooting Meg a questioning glance. You'd think after one day of a convenient marriage the novelty would've worn off, but it hadn't. She thought her body might pool up every time he came near.

"Ask him, Gary," she said.

Nick hooked his thumbs through his belt loops. Gary gulped. "My wife and I were wondering if you're both going to the Halloween charity dance."

Nick shrugged. Gary hadn't gotten on his good side yet.

The mellow lack of response seemed to fire Gary's courage. Maybe he figured Nick hadn't bothered to slap him upside the head, so it'd be okay to ask another pointless question.

"My wife was also wondering if Meg ate one of her own baby cakes to get herself with child."

Nick just stared. Even Meg felt a little uneasy with the intensity of his pale-blue glare.

With lightning speed, Gary scooted off his chair, leaving it spinning like a toy top. "Never mind."

And with a wild shiver of bells, they were alone.

"Your glares are more effective than a laser gun," said Meg. "I can't tell you how many months of ribbing I could've avoided with you around." She found herself twirling her wedding ring, a new anxious habit. It was as if she couldn't believe she was married and had to reassure herself that the diamonds and gold were real.

At that moment, a group of townspeople strolled by, gawking through the windows as if Meg and Nick were zoo animals. She fought the urge to lower her gaze, to passively accept the rudeness. But with Nick here, she felt strength. For some odd reason, she had the power to stand up for herself with him by her side.

They both stared down the passersby. The group looked away before Nick and Meg did. Small victory.

Nick turned to her. "Have you had to deal with that all day?"

Meg shed her apron and tucked it under the counter. "Word's out that we're married. We're the new headline in this town."

"Let's get you out of here."

She flushed, thinking of being alone at home with him. Thinking of the night she'd spent tossing and turning, just trying to forget that he was down the hall. "I need to clean up." She disappeared in the back.

When she finished closing, Nick helped her into the pickup, shielding her from the frankly curious stares from the good citizens of Kane's Crossing. Their condescending expressions felt like stones pelting her with malice.

What could she do to please them? She'd gotten married, for heaven's sake. You'd think that would've eased their moral disappointment in her.

Nick had slipped his shades back over his eyes, returning stare for stare from the people. As they drove out of town, they passed another of Chad's banners, this one filled with tiny holes.

Meg couldn't help laughing. "I wonder if Ashlyn took a BB gun to it."

He kept his attention on the road, resting a forearm on the steering wheel with casual grace. "Beats silverware or candlesticks for our wedding gift."

They hadn't really talked about Meg's impulsive decision to include Ashlyn in yesterday's ceremony. She thought that he'd been humoring her wedding-day jitters by not arguing the point. "I apologize for making things awkward by bringing her to the ceremony," she said.

"If you're thinking it'll encourage forgiveness, you're wrong."

Her chest felt hollow. She *had* been thinking along those lines. She wished his anger would disappear. "I'm sorry."

After a moment of strained silence, he reached over to skim a finger along her cheek. Meg couldn't hold back a tremble. Why did her body have to betray her better judgment?

"Don't apologize for trying to solve things." He concentrated on the road once again. "I have to take care of that myself."

The sentiment stirred up her loneliness. And she thought marriage was going to fill the empty places inside of her. No dice. "At any rate, don't expect to see Ashlyn around much. She just talks to me because it infuriates her family."

"Sort of an empty victory, huh? It reminds me of how you insist on working in that bakery day after day, serving those people."

His cutting words took her aback. "I like to stay busy, to create." She lifted her chin. "I plan to work until the day I have this baby."

He chuckled. "I don't think so."

Meg turned her body, tummy and all, toward him, skewering him with a glare. "Excuse me?"

"I've got money enough to last us a lifetime, Meggie. There's no need for you to slave for those people."

His voice, so low and rough, could've talked her into

anything, but his words set her on edge. "Thank you for the offer, but no thanks."

"Damn, you're stubborn."

"Always have been."

He waited a beat, then said, "You're my wife. Everything I have is yours."

Everything except your heart. She let the conversation die as she watched the sunset-hued trees swish by. They could argue about this later, but she wouldn't lower herself to take his money. She hadn't married him because she was digging for gold; she'd married him for the baby's sake. He didn't have to do her any more favors.

They pulled into the stand-alone garage on their property, entering the house in silence. The lingering scent of Aunt Valentine's magnolia perfume calmed her, made her feel as if her guardian were smoothing back her hair in a familiar gesture of comfort.

Nick went in one direction, she went in another. He'd asked permission to convert a downstairs guest bedroom into an office. Meg supposed he'd hole himself up in there in lieu of having to disagree with her again. She watched him shuck his leather jacket off those broad shoulders as he disappeared into the room.

Meg sighed and rubbed her stomach. Had it grown overnight? It felt bigger every day, along with her ankles, her face. Almost four more months of bloating and increased appetite. What a treat.

But she couldn't deny the pleasure that surged through her every time she rubbed her belly, imagining the baby cuddled beneath her palm. She'd told the doctor she didn't want to know the sex. It'd be a surprise to both her and its new father.

Meg only hoped he cared.

Well, she thought as she sauntered into the kitchen, she'd get at least one benefit from this marriage. She'd be able to raid Nick's closet for maternity clothes. Meg hadn't gone shopping yet—she knew she still had a major amount of weight to gain, oh joy—but she'd already pillaged Aunt Valentine's clothes in the attic since the elderly lady had carried a few more pounds than her niece.

Meg rubbed her eyes and debated whether or not it was worth the effort to actually cook dinner. Had Nick already eaten? She wasn't sure if she wanted to bother him in his present mood.

What sounded good? Pickles and ice cream? Right. She wasn't sure she'd even gone shopping this week for groceries. When she opened the refrigerator, she stepped back in shock. She knew she hadn't gone shopping for this stuff.

It was crammed with everything from buttermilk to meats to a garden spray of vegetables. With a sense of wonder, she peered at the kitchen table, laden with two place settings and a basket of whole-grain bread. Come to think of it, the room did smell a bit like tomato soup, chickpeas, carrots and beef. She wondered what was cooking in the oven.

Head cocked, Meg power-walked out of the kitchen straight to Nick's new office. He stood among a jungle of wires and machines: faxes, computer systems and phones.

"What is this?" she asked, referring to more than just the business center.

"Oh." He glanced around, as if miffed by the presence of the equipment. "I'll be working out of the house."

"Aunt Valentine would die a second time if she saw all these 'newfangled' monstrosities."

Nick smiled, tickling Meg's stomach. He glanced out the window, toward his view of the garden. "I don't think she'd mind so much."

Meg thought she felt her stomach gurgle. Food. "Did you do some shopping? Other than for this stuff?"

He looked away. "Yeah."

Before she could thank him he held up a finger. "Just give me a minute, and I'll get it ready for you."

Her stomach whirlpooled again. She slid both hands over the roundness, rubbing absently. His eyes followed her movements, then, as if thinking it was inappropriate for him to watch, he looked away and crossed his arms.

"I'll get it ready," he said after a moment, leaving the room.

Meg wandered over to the window, staring at a spot on the glass that resembled a ghost hovering over the garden.

There it was again. A little "pop!" in her stomach, like a kid blowing tiny bubbles with his gum. Meg inspected her shirt, thinking she'd find a tiny bug creeping around, causing the tickling sensation. No bug.

Was it the baby moving?

She choked up, tightening her grip on her belly, holding her breath to see if she was right.

Blip!

My Lord, it was her child.

She smiled and kept the information to herself, wondering if Nick would even blink an eye at the miracle of it all.

* * *

After dinner Nick took Meggie to the comfortable couch and ottoman to rest, then cleaned the kitchen. Although he'd always thought of himself as the servant boy in more than a few foster homes, he'd never taken such comfort from washing dishes and storing the food away. But now he felt as if he had a purpose—to keep Meggie safe.

He'd caught a glint of something mysterious in her eyes a time or two today, and he wondered if he was doing everything within his power to make her happy. Both of them had gone into this marriage knowing that it wasn't real, knowing that they'd never truly be husband and wife. He hoped Meggie wasn't forgetting that.

When he came out of the kitchen, he found Meggie staring out the front bay window at the dusky sky, the view of Kane's Crossing making him feel as if he could own the place. She seemed so pensive, so much younger than her twenty-eight years in her long-sleeved Henley shirt and a loose ponytail that hadn't confined all of her corkscrew hair. A few stray strands framed her face, softening it. She had her hands planted on her belly, slowly glissading them back and forth. It'd feel so good to put his hands over hers, to feel her heat.

He shook off the thought. ''Tired?''

She didn't look at him. ''You don't have to carry me up the stairs again.''

''Good news for my back.''

She smiled wickedly, then widened her eyes and stopped rubbing her stomach. When she looked at him again, there seemed to be a sheen of guilt in her gaze.

''What?'' he asked.

''Nothing.'' She turned back to the window.

Why did he feel as if she'd shut him out? Suddenly he felt like an outsider, a lonely little boy who didn't belong to anyone. A foster child who'd traipsed through too many doorways.

He left Meggie to her thoughts and went to his new office to work. Immediately, his blood started to pump. Nick was ready to purchase the Spencer Toy Factory near the outskirts of town. The factory where his foster father had been killed. He'd have that business in his possession soon, and it wouldn't stop there. He was ready to buy other Spencer properties, secretly, until he owned what they owned.

Hostile takeovers. Just as hostile as Chad had been when he'd set off that bomb, when he'd sent those poor families packing without any thought to their futures.

Nick had done enough work for the night. When he went in search of Meggie, he found her in the parlor, sitting on a lumpy quilt with her legs crossed, her arms stretched in the air. Her posture echoed the immense pipe organ behind her with its brass pipes blasting from the wood.

"Three point field goal?" he asked, not quite sure what she was doing.

Meggie exhaled. "Stretching exercises. You can't start too early."

It was all for the baby. A good father would offer to help. A good father wouldn't be afraid of insinuating himself into his child's life. Nick wanted to ask if there was anything he could do for her, but his tongue stilled. He'd had a lot of practice at staying silent.

In his mind's eye, he saw a small boy cowering in a corner, the shadow of a hand poised above him, ready to strike. *Be seen and not heard.*

Meggie had stopped, her arms hovering by her sides. "Are you all right, Nick?"

He nodded.

She looked at him, head cocked. "Looks like you just saw a ghost."

God, he wanted to touch her, to wind his finger inside one of her red curls and watch it bounce back when he set it free. He wanted to lay her down on the quilt, to lift her shirt and explore the crescent of her body, the swell of her breasts. He could imagine burying his nose in her neck, how it'd remind him of strawberry fields and sunshine.

He hadn't experienced much sun in his life, and now that he had the chance, he was blowing it. But he hadn't married Meggie to seduce her. He needed to remain focused on why he'd come to Kane's Crossing in the first place.

He hooked his thumbs in his belt loops. "Is there anything I can do for you before I go to sleep?"

Somehow he felt that question held more meaning than he'd originally intended. Meggie's blush told him that any double entendres hadn't escaped her notice.

"I'm fine. Thanks...for the meal, for everything."

"Yeah." He started toward the stairs, then backtracked, holding out his hands to help Meggie to her feet.

She grinned gratefully and latched onto him. There they stood, toe to toe, almost body to body, just staring at each other, wondering what could come next if they allowed it.

Meggie shut her eyes, breaking the moment. It seemed as if she were in some pain. Nick realized that she was holding her back.

"Extra-wide load," she said.

His hands itched to make it better, to smooth down the slope of her back until they reached the small.

Nick mentally rolled his eyes and gave in. He led her to the ottoman. "Take a seat."

"Why?" asked Meggie, eyes wide.

"You need a helping hand."

And as she sat, Nick cursed under his breath. Giving his wife a massage was probably the worst idea he'd had since he'd laid eyes on her.

Meg's back ached something fierce, as if someone were punching ten thousand pins into her tailbone. Usually she tried to bear her pains with stoic ambivalence; after all, backaches came with the pregnancy territory. But Nick had caught on right away. Had she been so dramatic?

He'd sat her on the velvet ottoman so she faced the empty fireplace, its marble mantel stretched across dark wallpaper like the pale arms of someone inching along her walls, trying to hide, and finding zero success. Aunt Valentine had lovingly placed Giuseppe Armani figurines on the mantel: brides, roaring twenties belles, carefree women in show-girl satin, all frozen in dance. The collectibles seemed to wink at Meg as if saying, "Brighten up, girl. Your husband's about to put his hands on you."

Oh, boy, her husband. Nick.

The first touch of his palm, warm and firm, slid over her backbone with a surprising gentleness. Meg felt a shiver fly through her.

"Cold?" he asked, removing his hand. "I can fix a fire."

She was hardly freezing. Hot, more likely. So hot she wanted to grab his hand and lead him to places she'd only fantasized about him touching. "No, no. I'm fine. We've got the central heating."

Without a word, he applied pressure again, using his strong fingers to knead her skin and muscle. She found herself moving with his ministrations, and she stiffened in protest.

"You're tense," he said, a worried undercurrent to his tone.

Tell me about it. She needed to remember this wasn't a real marriage, that they were friends. "I'm fine."

"Being stressed can't be good for the baby."

His hands never left her body as she felt him sit on the couch behind her, heard his shallow breathing, closed her eyes due to the headiness of his leathery scent.

"I wish you'd relax, Meggie."

His voice was low, as melodic as the sounds of a summer night. It sang to her, puckering her skin with goose bumps in reaction to the feel of his words tickling the nape of her exposed neck.

This was crazy. She was nuts for ever having accepted Nick's marriage offer in light of the way Chad had treated her. "I can take care of myself, Nick. Don't you remember?"

He chuckled, his touch stilling for a brief instant. "Yeah. I remember."

"What's so funny?"

He started massaging again. "I can still see you, little Meggie Thornton, with your rock-and-roll skirt outfit, chasing after Chad Spencer when he took that long stick and lifted the material."

He would have to bring that up. It'd been the first time Nick had talked with her, had even acknowledged her existence. She'd seen him around a couple of times—he'd just moved to Kane's Crossing under the mysterious guise of "that foster kid"—but they'd never even made eye contact. Then, that one day near the end of summer, Chad had been teasing her at the drive-in hamburger stop by the highway. Meg had been hanging out with older friends, avoiding Chad, his friends and their mind-in-the-gutter smiles. Without her knowing, he'd sneaked up behind her with a stick pilfered from the road edge and, bit by bit, started lifting her skirt until every kid at the drive-in had gotten a gander at her rainbow-branded undies.

Nobody had really noticed Nick was there until she'd run after Chad, driving him straight into the solid wall of Nick's body. "The frightening freshman," that's how everyone referred to him. And Nick had made good on his name by grabbing the offensive stick, tossing it away as if it were as light as a toothpick and glaring down into Chad's ashen face.

Nobody fooled with her the rest of the vacation. She'd gone home to San Diego and returned the next summer, becoming best friends with Nick Cassidy. And then he'd left amid the smoke of an explosion....

She chased away the memory. Nick had said he wasn't the one who'd committed the crime. Did she believe him?

Absolutely. His intentions had always been noble, never base or cruel. This was a man she would've been able to trust had her heart not already been smashed to pieces.

Her answering laugh came out weak, strained. "Chad wasn't used to people correcting his behavior. His parents never even checked him. He was always Mister Perfect, Mister My-Boy-Would-Never-Do-That."

She felt Nick's fingers lose their rhythm, then get back into sync. "Don't take offense, Meggie, you don't have to answer this. How the hell did you and Spencer ever end up together?"

Excellent question. "Do you really want to hear my tale of woe?"

Softly. "Yeah."

She took a breath, exhaled, relaxed into Nick's hands.

"Aunt Valentine knew she was dying. She'd gotten slower within the past year—no more bustling around the house with all that excess energy. She tried to prepare me for her death, but I wouldn't believe it." Meg choked on the next words. "I was so afraid of her leaving me."

She cleared her throat. "But Aunt Valentine was so happy, as if she knew exactly what would happen to her after she died. She always told me to wish her well at her last breath."

Meg stopped for a moment, wavering under Nick's hands and the images of her aunt reclining peacefully in her favorite wing chair, the golden upholstery making her face seem saintly, angelic before its time. "I found her, of course. She'd gone like a sunset, so quietly. It looked like she was just sleeping. But she wouldn't wake up." Meg's throat burned.

"She wouldn't wake up," she repeated, whispering.

Nick had run his palms up her back to cup her shoulders. He gripped her reassuringly, giving her strength to continue.

Meg sighed and lifted her chin. "After I took care of all the arrangements, a couple of people sent condolences. Chad sent dozens of flowers, and I almost fainted from surprise. He'd never been civil to me, just always lascivious. A dog.''

''So what made you think his sentiments were genuine?''

''I really don't know. I didn't buy his act at first. I thought there was some ulterior motive behind this kindness.''

Nick's grip told her that she didn't need to mention that there was something more to Chad's motivation. If anyone knew, it was Nick.

She continued. ''He caught me in town one day. I was still wearing black, even if that's old-fashioned. Anyway, he was so nice, so unlike Chad ever was. He explained that he'd changed since high school, that he'd come back from college a new man.''

''Right.''

''I'm far too trusting sometimes.''

Nick's fingers brushed over her hair, a caring, tender gesture that almost tore out her heart. ''That's why you're Meggie. Trust makes you good.''

''It makes you let down your guard.'' Memories, as gray as a chain of empty days, flashed through her mind. ''I was scared to death of being by myself the rest of my life. Chad made promises, and I didn't know any better than to believe them. He courted me for a bit, pulled out all the romantic stops. I really thought he cared.''

She'd been pretty inexperienced as far as men were concerned. She'd been too busy taking care of Aunt Valentine and the bakery, too busy hiding in their house on the hill from all the stares and insults. Too busy waiting for true love to come to *her*.

Too bad she'd thought Chad would provide comfort and love. Too bad she'd believed his hollow words.

"I was with him only that one night."

Nick flinched and took his touch away, leaving her cold. As cold as the ashes of Chad's lovemaking.

Of course Nick was disappointed in her. Chad had ruined Nick's life, and she'd done the ultimate intimate act with his enemy. The bitter irony made her as ill as Nick must've been.

"I know you must be so disgusted with me right now," she said, crossing her arms over her chest and rubbing for warmth. "But I got my just deserts. He didn't even stay the whole night. You see, he was going to Europe the next day, and he thought he'd just give himself a good going-away present. I even remember his last words before he scooted out the door. 'Everyone always dared me to nail the witch. It wasn't as bad as I expected.'"

Meg bolted out of her seat, away from Nick. Away from the awful glare he must've been boring into her back. She stared at the mantel figurines, wishing she could be as peaceful as they seemed.

She heard him rise from the couch, heard his boot heels scuff across the carpet until they came to within inches of where she stood.

He didn't even say anything, just gathered her into his strong arms to hold her close. Then, with the softest wing-flutter of a touch, he skimmed his lips over her forehead. A burst of heat and contentment, of relief and acceptance coursed through her veins, clogging her chest, making her want to explode into tears right in front of him.

"No worries, Meggie," he whispered, soft and low, making her wonder what in the world she'd done to deserve his protection.

No worries....

* * *

After Nick had walked Meggie up to her room, he'd come straight outside to stare at the tiny pond by Valentine's garden. Every minute or so, he'd flip a pebble into the water, just to watch the surface shiver with ripples.

Words. Each pebble was like a word, disrupting the flow of things. A carefully tossed stone didn't cause much harm. If he were to throw one with force, as he'd done when he'd first come outside, there'd be a mighty splash. Damage. Spots that wouldn't disappear for ages to come.

He wished he could've been here for Meggie in her time of need. He felt guilty, as if sleeping on the job. What if he'd come to Kane's Crossing more than five months ago to provide comfort for her? Would Meggie have slept with Chad?

He was far from feeling angry with her, as he'd been upon first entering town. He'd felt betrayed. But not anymore. Now he just felt sickened by Chad's careless words and actions.

It was the last time the golden boy would cause any damage.

The nine o'clock sky had cleared and turned a deep blue. He wasn't really tired, just bone-weary. Not the same thing.

Might as well go up to bed. You could only throw stones for so long before it all became an exercise in futility.

He tried to keep the kitchen screened door from slapping against the frame as he walked inside. Still, the slight chop echoed through the mammoth house. He stood for a moment, trying to detect some movement to match the energy he felt humming around him. Call him bonkers, but he thought he could smell that magnolia scent again.

He waved a hand in front of his face, a true skeptic.

It'd been a hard night, especially for Meggie. He hoped the stress hadn't hurt the baby.

The baby? Did he care so much?

Nick didn't want to admit to anything, so he cleared his mind and headed up the creaking stairway, down the hall, his boots laying heavy on the old wood. The worn burgundy carpet didn't cushion any of the sound as he walked past Meggie's room.

He stopped in front of her door, as he'd done last night. Propping a hand against the wall, he thought about what rested behind the doorway: a long, foggy mirror with sheer purple material draped over the top and sides, crystal balls shining on nightstands and dressers, a canopy bed with filmy netting swooping between the wooden posts, a newly formed life slumbering in a womb and strawberry curls relaxing over the white of a pillowcase.

His hands itched to touch her again. It'd felt good to press them against her back. What would it have felt like to cup around the front, lightly kneading the round of her stomach? Slipping upward to palm her breasts?

Would she moan with longing? Or would she glare at him as if he were one of the boys—the same club as Chad Spencer?

Dammit, he didn't have the time or the inclination for this idiocy. He'd come to Kane's Crossing for the purpose of serving it up to Spencer, and that's how it'd stay.

He'd be damned if he became emotionally involved beyond giving Meggie and her child a name.

Chapter Six

A week later, after many more stops and starts in front of Meggie's bedroom, Nick had summoned up enough courage to persuade her to come to the town's Halloween charity dance. It was time for them to make a public appearance.

Meggie had gone inside Willowbreeze House, which had opened its antebellum doors to serve refreshments. She'd told Nick that she needed to perk up in the powder room, but he knew better. Her voice had been trembling when she said it; she was nervous.

He cursed at himself for bringing her tonight. Hadn't he wanted to lower her stress level? But, after he'd brought up the subject, she insisted. She was just as tired as he was of being on the outside of society. Tonight, they were going in.

He held a bottle-necked glass of beer between his fingers, leaning his elbow against the plank-board countertop of the Moose Lodge's snack booth. The ladies' auxiliary had strung white bulb lights through the trees of Pioneer Square, giving the jack-o'-lantern-strewn grounds a starlight glow. Black-and-orange banners fluttered over booth tops and the roof of the latticed gazebo that formed the park's hub. Inside, a band played, complete with rat-ta-tat drums, trombones, trumpets, flutes and clarinets. Nick expected the Music Man to pop in to lead their turn-of-the-century repertoire at any moment.

Not surprisingly, Chad Spencer's presence had made itself known, compliments of Spencer High School's athletic department. Blown up black-and-white posterboard pictures showcased Chad in his all-state football uniform, an accompanying placard boasting his stats for his senior year as quarterback. Several more pictures featured college numbers and poses. It was obvious that Chad was this town's favorite son.

We Miss You, screamed a banner that floated over Nick's head.

He clenched his jaw and clutched his bottle.

"Haven't you charmed the crowds yet?"

Meggie had sneaked up behind him, and he stood a little straighter in her presence.

Since this was a Halloween function, everyone wore masks and costumes. Meggie had elected to dress as an angel, and it wasn't a far stretch of the imagination. But she wasn't just your garden-variety specter in white. No, she'd used a burgundy-velvet cape with gold trim and embroidery with a sunset lining, topping a dress of the same colors, overlaid with wispy earth-hued material. Her curly hair had grown longer since he'd first come to town, more lustrous, and she'd threaded golden flowers through it, reminding Nick of their wedding day. Petite, translucent wings capped her back, and a shiny golden sun mask covered most of her face, completing the costume.

He caught his breath. ''I thought you'd hiked back home, Ms. Independent Spirit.''

''I almost did when I realized you weren't kidding about not dressing in a costume.'' She cocked her head. ''You could've at least worn a mask to get into the swing of things.''

He hooked one thumb into a belt loop, peering at the rest of the crowd: the clowns, the tigers, the princesses. No way anyone would ever make him wear a mask. ''Ready to brave the consequences?''

He crooked out an arm, and Meggie slipped a hand between his leather-clad biceps and forearm. She lifted her chin.

''Let's go.''

That was his woman, able to face a challenge anyday. He couldn't wait for Spencer to see how she'd gotten over him.

It was pretty surreal to walk into a throng of people and leave silence behind. Nick thought the experience could be compared to the parting of the Red Sea. Shock will do that to folks, make them freeze like mindless statues and stare without a thought to manners.

He thought it might be fun to greet the head of Spencer's fan club—the ladies' auxiliary—first.

Mrs. Spindlebund's spine stiffened approximately twelve feet before Nick and Meggie stood in front of her booth. He couldn't hold back a smile. When he was young, she'd enjoyed screeching like a crow at him whenever he'd walked by her house on the way home. He couldn't remember why she'd yelled so much, but, even now, she was just as red in the face.

He cleared his throat, waiting for her to look him in the eye. He nodded in greeting to the elderly woman.

She peered through the eyeholes of her half-mask at his beer. "A little strong, don't you think, Mr. Cassidy?"

"Not strong enough." He saluted her with the bottle and took a healthy swig.

Meggie's hand tightened on his arm before she spoke. "The decorations are lovely."

"Of course they are. Mr. Cassidy, I assume you're not here to cause trouble tonight? We've gone through a lot of work to make this function a success, what with the charity money going to the memorial and all."

"Memorial?" asked Meggie, speaking for him, as well.

Mrs. Spindlebund's bat ears slipped from her salt-and-pepper hair. "For Kane Spencer, founder of our town. Meghan Thornton, don't you attend any town meetings?"

Nick bristled. "That's Meghan Cassidy now."

The elderly woman's lips tightened into a straight-arrow line before she said, "So I've heard."

The clang of a game bell sounded behind them, followed by a chorus of cheers. Nick nodded his head in Mrs. Spindlebund's direction. It was no secret he'd never been one to waste words, but now was a good time to spend some. "I think we'll appreciate your club's backbreaking work. After all, it's for a good cause." He couldn't help the ironic grin that crossed his mouth as he stepped away from the booth.

As they moved on, Meggie whispered, "I see you're not out to make friends tonight."

"Am I ever?"

Meggie shook her head. "Maybe I could volunteer your services in the dunking tank, Nick."

He stopped their progress to run a finger over her soft cheek. She blushed and peered at the ground.

They were interrupted by a loud snicker. A diminutive lion pounced to their sides. "You said hi to Spindlebund? Are you brave."

"Hi, Gary," they both said in unison.

Their moment was broken. Suddenly, Nick just wanted to take Meggie home and hold her in his arms, keeping her secure from everything in this park.

"Boy, Meg," Gary said, "you're a real beaut of an angel. Isn't she, Nick?"

"Where's your wife?" Where was anyone who could keep Gary Joanson away from them? If Nick didn't know any better, he'd have thought the irritating man actually liked them.

"Aw, she's off cheetering with the other women about the new gossip. You all hear about the Spencers' factory being bought?"

Nick tried to look nonchalant, but he noticed that Meggie slid a sidelong glance in his direction. He merely shrugged.

Gary puffed up his chest, the bearer of important news. "No one knows who owns it now, and I can tell you that the Spencers ain't too happy about it, either. Some kind of hospitable takeover."

"Hostile," murmured Meg.

It'd been easier than that, actually. Now Nick had his eye on buying the Mercantile Department Store, the pride of the Spencer family's retail holdings. As a matter of fact, Nick had realized that Kane's Crossing held many opportunities for fortune. Take the abandoned property by Cutter's Lake, for instance. The location would be perfect for a shopping/amusement arcade.

Nick wondered how many people were buzzing with the information about the factory. What would they do if they knew he owned it now? They'd all choke on their judgmental tongues, that's what they'd do. But it wasn't time to reveal himself yet—not until he could buy back the houses that belonged to the displaced families.

"Whatever it is," continued Gary, full of steam from his story, "the workers are running around like scared chickens."

Nick would have to find a way to reassure the workers that their jobs weren't in jeopardy. "Any other earth-shattering news?" Casual, just be casual.

Gary shrugged. "Not that I know of."

So they hadn't caught wind of the purchase of his foster family's old house. Good. That would stay a secret for a while.

Meg stirred next to him. "Gary, you sure seem to be chipper about this piece of gossip."

The little man shrank back. "Me? Oh, no. Just something to talk about."

Was that fear behind his mask? Just as Nick was about to further explore that possibility, Gary jumped, his lion's tale springing up and down with incredible animation.

"I gotta go." And he was off in a flash.

Nick followed his progress, narrowing his eyes when he saw where Gary was heading.

Sonny Jenks and Junior Crabbe huddled by a throw-the-dart booth, staring daggers at their approaching crony. Gary glanced over his shoulder at Nick and Meg, adjusting his walk to a bull-legged swagger as he neared his crowd. As he joined them, he never looked back.

Nick shook his head. He felt Meggie tug on his arm.

"I could really use a glass of lemonade."

He smiled down at her, willing to fulfill her every wish. They strolled past cake-walk games, catch-the-goldfish challenges and a makeshift haunted house framed by skittish children who tittered every time one of their friends screamed out of the blanket that served as a door. Moans, thunder and clanking chains could be heard behind the mysterious partition.

After buying the lemonade from the high school's home ec club, Nick found Meggie a seat on a bench beneath a willow tree. A hobo slouched at the other end.

Nick finished his beer and tossed the bottle into a waiting container. "That Gary's a character."

"One with some pretty good information."

She'd discarded her mask, and when he met Meggie's eyes, they were wary.

"Do you know anything about that factory?" she asked.

He opened his mouth to answer, not that he knew what the response would be. Luckily, the lump at the end of the bench spoke before he could.

"Factory was the mainstay of the Spencers' income. Whoever bought it didn't do it with their blessing." The hobo looked up, and a string of lights filtered bright dots across Deacon Chaney's face. Nick realized that the old man wasn't even wearing a costume.

"You know an awful lot about the Spencers," said Nick.

Deacon leaned back and tucked his hands into his frayed pockets. "I know more than I care to."

The man still hadn't made eye contact with him, but at least he was speaking. Nick wanted to say something—anything—that would inform Chaney that he wasn't the one who'd blown up his drugstore. But Nick had his pride. He wouldn't grovel, dammit.

Meggie must've sensed his prickly mood. "What do you say we play a game or two."

Nick helped her to her feet, taking care to avoid Chaney.

Meggie walked over to the old man, putting a hand on his shoulder. "Take care, Mr. Chaney. Stay warm."

He didn't say a word as they walked away. When they were a safe enough distance, Nick muttered, "He's as stubborn as the day is long."

"He's suffered through a lot, Nick. He'll come around, you just wait."

She smiled up at him, her clear green eyes making his heart do ridiculous, schoolkid stomps. *Steer clear, guy, steer clear.*

As they wandered through Pioneer Square, a few citizens actually stopped to congratulate them on their wedding. Every time someone talked, however, Nick sensed a thread of fear hiding in their voices, just behind their eyes. Why, he didn't know. But he couldn't help wondering which one of these people would be the next to lose their homes to Chad Spencer.

Music filtered through the crisp air, urging Nick to grab Meggie's hand. When he heard her intake of breath, he looked at their joined fingers, wondering what had propelled him to be so…impetuous. The last time he'd held a woman's hand had been back when he'd run around Kane's Crossing with Meggie, and even then, it'd been more of a "Come on, let's go!"

gesture. This was different. He couldn't explain why, but it just was.

He looked at the makeshift dance floor and grinned. What the hell. They were married, right? Why shouldn't they let Kane's Crossing know it?

He looked into her eyes. "We never did have a wedding dance."

The gazebo-turned-bandstand shimmered with the glint of brass from instruments and band uniforms. Meg wanted more than anything to give in to her longings and cuddle into Nick's arms, but she didn't want to do it in front of all these people.

Well, that was the point, wasn't it? To pose in front of the community, to show everyone she wasn't a pregnant single mother anymore? She wondered if they believed that Nick could be the father of her baby. Maybe she needed to do all she had to, to keep her secret.

"Are you issuing an invitation, Nick?" She couldn't help the flutter of her eyelashes.

His gaze went from her eyes to her mouth and lingered for an extended second. Good, a reaction. He actually seemed as if he'd lost himself for a moment there.

He thumbed over the slope of her index finger and lightly pulled her to the dance floor. The band, culled from retired shopkeepers and factory workers, swept into a forties tune, one that recalled moonlight, Pearl Harbor and dahlia-soft glamour.

He led her into his body, her protruding stomach grooving next to his. With every swish of contact, her blood boiled a little hotter. After they'd settled into a rhythm, Nick took her hand and placed it behind his neck, so both her hands rested there, itching to play with slight earth-toned curls rebelling at his neckline.

She was feeling way too dizzy, way too lost. In a bid to keep the moment light, she said, "Why'd you have to provoke Mrs. Spindlebund?"

"Who, me?" he murmured.

The music was so soft, so romantic, she wanted to just shut up and dance. But that would be dangerous. If she came to believe that Nick had married her for more than pity, she'd be in for heartbreak. "Yeah, you. Did you think she was going to leap up and embrace the prodigal son of this town?"

He grinned and watched the other dancers. Meg turned his face back to her, her fingers wisping against stubble.

"As far as these people remember, you were a criminal. When are you going to let them know you didn't set off that bomb?"

"Maybe I should seize the microphone and make an announcement to the hordes."

"Maybe you should." She sighed. "It's better than poking your finger into dark holes, hoping you won't get bitten."

"I'll be fine, Meggie." His hands crept beneath her cape, smoothing over her back, tugging her closer to him. She could feel the ridges of his body, all sinew and heat. Her swollen, sensitive breasts pressed into his hard chest, making her all but choke with the rush of longing that filled her. This didn't feel too "friendly."

Meg pushed back from him a tad. "I don't understand you at all."

Grin aside, his expression became serious. "Maybe that's for the best."

She didn't answer. She might've choked if she

would've tried. A husband who didn't want to be personal. Wasn't that just her luck? Then again, she had to admit, he was doing the right thing. Getting personal, sharing life as a real married couple, would only make their business arrangement harder. He'd never promised her anything more.

All the same, she still wanted to know what he knew about the Spencers' factory being purchased by another party. She thought of his computers, faxes, phones, millions…

Forget it. Nick would never take his anger far enough to ruin someone else's life. Would he?

"Nick…?"

They almost came to a standstill right in the middle of the dance floor, among a bunch of strangers. Her friend Rachel wouldn't step foot at a Kane's Crossing function, and Ashlyn, the next closest thing to a friendly face in this town, wouldn't ever help to raise money for such a vain memorial by attending this party. That left a bunch of masked, curious faces, watching, wondering. Not exactly a hotbed of comfort.

"Are you okay, Meggie?" He used his knuckles to sift over her cheek, and she fought the need to burrow into his touch.

He had the same look on his face that she'd seen at the county clerk's when they'd married each other. The damn-it-all, slightly beaten expression that'd come right before they'd kissed each other. Was he going to kiss her now? Out in public?

They stopped dancing, and she stared into his morning-sky eyes. Then, as he moved closer, bringing the scent of musk and leather with him, her lids fluttered, blocking her gaze altogether. She felt the sandpaper friction of his chin dragging over her jawline, his rough cheek scratching against hers. His mouth rested just above hers.

"Do we look married enough for them?" he whispered, lips breathing over lips with the barest of pressure.

She shuddered, a thousand watts of electricity bouncing against her skin, digging underneath, making her grab onto his jacket to keep her balance. So what if he was doing this for appearances? The moment was hers to hold and shape any way she wanted to.

Until reality struck.

She backed up, taking a deep breath of him before depriving herself. "I'm tired, Nick." *Tired of worrying, of trying to throw these hounds off my scent.*

He nodded and adjusted his jacket around his throat. "Let's get you home."

He grabbed her hand, and, just like that, they were back to being the teenagers who ran from stream to stream, savoring their time together. So many places to see, so many feelings to experience. At least, that's what she'd thought all those years ago.

They were in the parking lot when a creaky, twanging voice stopped their progress. "Hey, Witchy Poo, if ya turned that angel costume inside out, would ya get a demon dress?"

Sonny Jenks. Junior Crabbe. The gang, including Gary Joanson, tail between legs.

They were leaning against Nick's pickup without a thought to paint jobs or propriety. One of them even held a stone that was poised for damage.

"Come on, guys," she said, falling back into her usual peacemaker mode. "It's late. We'd like to leave without a hassle."

Nick stepped in front of her, using his body as a shield. "You never got past high school, did you?"

"Oo-ha," yelled Junior, who wore a yellowed sheet around his shoulders in a failed attempt to be ghostlike. "That boy grew a mouth."

Sonny sniffed. "Won't do him much good when that mouth connects to my fist."

"So that's how it is," said Nick, his voice a low rumble. "I guess it'd have to be physical with you, Sonny, seeing as you'd come to a battle of wits unarmed."

Meg wanted to stop it all, but she knew that if she said anything more, it would undermine Nick's ability to defend himself. He wanted respect. She'd have to give him room to earn some.

She allowed him to stand in front of her, to protect her and her baby.

Junior laughed and pushed Gary to the forefront. "Don't go haywire on us, Cassidy. All we want to know is if it's true." He poked at Gary. "Go ahead, tell 'em."

Gary's face was red under his fading face paint. With the little space she had, Meg could see he was doing his best to maintain some dignity. "I told them you were the dad of Meg's baby."

"And we think that's a load of cock and bull," piped Sonny.

At this, Meg's body tightened with fear. Couldn't they just leave the subject alone?

Nick was silent, no doubt using his stare of death. It worked on everyone except Sonny.

"You heard me, Cassidy. Are you the daddy?"

Meg could see Nick's shoulders bunch under his

jacket, his feet move apart in gunfighter stance. Sonny was in for it.

Respect or not, she wouldn't let him jump three-to-one into a fistfight. "Just let it go," she whispered.

He turned his face in profile to her, his jaw firm. Half his features were in shadow, casting him in a light so threatening, even she wanted to run. His hands hovered near his hips, ready for action. "It's not right, Meggie. They can't get away with talking to you like that."

"But I don't care." He'd know she was lying, that was the worst of it. She cared more than anything about keeping her baby from Chad. And Nick would make sure everyone thought he was the father, even if it meant using his fists to do the convincing.

Sonny spoke up. "Can't decide who Daddy is, Witchy Poo? Too many choices?"

Nick moved with the grace and speed of a flying bullet. The cronies scattered as he found his mark in Sonny, pinning him to the pickup cab with one nearly imperceptible motion. Meg sucked in her breath, hoping he hadn't started a death match.

Nick used a forearm to hold Sonny against the truck and used his other hand to clutch Sonny's ear between his thumb and forefinger, growling low in his throat. "You didn't learn the first time, did you, Sonny? She wasn't my wife then, but she sure is now. If you care to enlighten us with any more of your opinions, I suggest you go to hell to do it."

"Yeah, but...ouch...ouch...ouch..."

Nick twisted Sonny's ear, and Meg bit her lip, watching the other men. They were wobbling on their boot heels, possibly using their peanut brains to calculate the odds of successfully dog-piling Nick. Gary distanced himself from the two others, hanging back and watching Meg.

Nick continued. "Had enough fun?"

A burst of light flooded the area, and Sonny jumped away from Nick, rubbing the side of his head. The sheriff's patrol car pulled up, shining a searchlight over the activity.

"Everything all right, here?" asked Sheriff Carson, sticking his mottled face out the window.

Meg could see Nick's hackles rise at the sight of the sheriff, the same man who'd escorted him out of town years ago.

"Just fine, Sheriff," said Sonny, waving to the older man.

Sheriff Carson let loose a stream of brown spittle, the mess landing a half inch from Nick's boots. Nick's hands fisted.

"Get the tar out of here, Sonny, before I call your Ma. Jehoshaphat, you'd think you'd grow some sense by the age of thirty."

Sonny and the gang grinned sheepishly and shuffled out of the spotlight. Meg had no doubt the confrontation would continue on another fine day.

Nick wasn't looking at the sheriff. Meg thought it would've been like staring a nightmare in the face.

"That you, Nick Cassidy?"

He nodded.

"I thought I ran you outta town years ago. Even kicked dogs have sense enough not to come back." *Spi-iit.* Another arch of tobacco landed near Nick's feet, closer this time. He didn't flinch.

Meg stepped into the light. "Sheriff Carson, there's no trouble. Just Sonny and Junior causing mischief."

"You'd know about mischief, girl."

She kept her tongue, feeling shame creep over her like a breath-robbing shroud.

The sheriff stared a moment longer. "You stay outta the town's business, Cassidy. That's all I have to say on the matter."

Gravel crunched under tires as the sheriff rode away, keeping the spotlight on them until he rounded a corner. They didn't move the entire time.

She could hear Nick breathing heavily. "Don't listen to anyone here, Nick. I—"

He rounded on his truck, throwing a punch into the window. The glass shattered into thousands of tiny slivers, a spiderweb of anger, but it didn't break; it merely buckled inward under the pressure.

"Nick!"

He hesitated, still as midnight, then finally opened the door, checked the interior and brushed some glass from the seat with his other hand. "Your side's fine. Let's go."

She paused a beat, then went around to her seat, trying to catch a glimpse of his fist. He'd capped it with his other hand, hiding the damage from her.

As he drove home with one hand on the steering wheel, Meg shouldered into the passenger door, as far from him as space would allow.

She didn't know if she could live with her husband's anger.

Chapter Seven

Nick rested his wounded hand on the backyard workshop bench before he continued his mission.

Even though he'd foolishly injured the appendage a few days ago, it still throbbed. But the real pain was more mental than physical. His conscience had sustained more shattered damage than the window had, due to the expression of disgust and shock on Meggie's face the night of the charity dance.

He absently tugged at the loose bandages swathing the injuries and thought about Meggie cowering in the corner of his pickup, Meggie shrinking into the house woodwork once they'd returned home. She'd asked him if she could tend to his wounds, but he'd refused, turning his back on her. The soft thumps of her slow walk up the staircase had hammered his heart, bruising it with guilt.

You'd think he'd hit her instead of the window. The

mere thought made him shudder. He'd do his damnedest to make sure he never lost control like that again. Violence wasn't the answer—it wouldn't bring him justice. Revenge was a matter of deliberate, methodical planning. His outburst of rage had only emphasized that fact.

Everyone who'd ever doubted him would see that he'd made good. That was a certainty.

In the meantime, he'd need to make it up to Meggie. He couldn't stand the way she'd been avoiding his presence the past few days. He'd even offered to help her with those odd exercises she did on her blanket in front of the pipe organ, but she'd turned him down flat, as if dreading his touch.

Maybe this would be a start, he thought, grabbing a varnish-smudged cloth and resuming work on his next project.

An old-fashioned cradle. He'd found it in one of the vacant rooms of this old house. That was the one of the beauties of living here—something new was always popping up in unexpected places. Nick and Meggie had found everything from a candy-red, mint-conditioned Radio Flyer wagon to what Meggie told him was a delicate, Belgian-lace christening gown, all just tucked patiently into one of the lone corners in the mothball-scented rooms.

This particular find would take some attention. It also needed a new coat of paint and a night or two of reweaving the wicker on the hood. Then he'd do something about the interior, stuffing a new mini-mattress, if need be.

He hoped it would bring a shine to Meggie's eyes.

Nick shook his head, taking the cloth to the dull cradle exterior. Making his wife happy had become more important than anything else in his life, and it threw him off balance. He'd never spent more than a month or two with the same woman. He'd just moved from girlfriend to girlfriend, place to place, drifting like smoke on the wind, never settling or becoming whole.

He couldn't believe he was locked in one place now. Well, it wouldn't be for too long. Meggie would have her freedom after he made sure Chad Spencer was ruined financially. Then he could buy her a house with a big garden—one with all the colors of a child's dreams—out of state where she could raise her child in peace and anonymity, away from Spencer. She didn't need Nick Cassidy to be happy.

Nick knew he was a damned hypocrite, but he couldn't help the need to keep Meggie safe from a vile person like Spencer... Even if he was planning to rub his marriage to Meggie in Spencer's face. Something selfish in Nick wanted his nemesis to see that he had what Spencer didn't.

Nick hardened his heart as guilt set in, knowing that he was doing what was best for his wife in the end. Although he intended to stay married only for the amount of time it took for Meggie to be free of Spencer, he was doing the right thing. But he'd have to make sure he didn't become too involved with her and the unborn baby; she probably wouldn't even want him around, anyway, after she found out how deep his hate simmered.

After he made sure Meggie was safe and sound in her own home outside of Kane's Crossing, Nick could scratch the itch to find his foster brother, Sam Reno. Sam was the only family left whom Nick cared to see. It nagged at his mind that his older brother thought he was a criminal. Sam's opinion mattered the most, even if everyone in Kane's Crossing ended up believing he wasn't a crook.

A whoosh of the night wind caused Nick to raise his head from his efforts. He hadn't realized he'd been working so late. He wanted to check on Meggie.

Nick washed up, ran his uninjured hand through his hair and sauntered back to the main house, which resembled a dark cloud on the horizon. Strange silhouettes crept down the hill to the front gate. What the hell?

Nick rushed through the kitchen door, wondering who'd come to visit.

"Meggie, who…?"

She was stretched out on the floor, stomach balling toward the ceiling, a glass with a mist of white-milk shadow near her head. Her hands rubbed against her belly, as if she was conjuring images from a crystal ball.

"Who what?" she said, as if this was the most normal position in the world.

He forgot his first question. "*What* are you doing?"

There was that guilty look again, the one she got when he caught her touching her stomach. What was running through her mind?

"Oo-oh," she said, eyes widening. "I felt it."

"What?"

For a minute, it looked as if she wasn't going to let him in on the secret. Then she relented. "The baby. I can feel him or her moving. Just a little. It's like when someone is fooling around and they put their lips on your cheek and blow so the skin buzzes."

He couldn't stop himself from kneeling at her side. Before he thought to ask permission, he placed his palm over her stomach, filling his hand with another life. "I don't feel anything."

"Just wait."

They sat in the same position for what seemed like an eternity. Somehow it felt right, that he was the one feeling the child. Not that he'd ever be able to fully embrace any part of Chad Spencer, but he was content to play daddy when Meggie needed him most.

There. A tiny vibration, a gurgle. "Damn, I feel it!"

"Don't cuss in front of the baby."

He grinned. "Sorry, Mom."

They locked gazes for a moment, unspoken words zapping in the space between, as he kept his hand on her stomach. How had he gotten so comfortable with this situation?

Meggie struggled to her elbows, forcing him to remove his hand. "Show's over. I think baby's done amusing us for the night."

He felt his hand travel upward again, moving toward her body.

The doorbell rang, jolting him out of his stupor. He remembered the question he'd come here to ask. "Who's at our door?"

"Trick-or-treaters. It's Halloween, remember?"

That's right. He'd been so caught up in his own activities that he'd forgotten to watch the world go by. "I thought I saw someone walking down the hill."

Meggie cocked her eyebrow. "Kids. They didn't even knock, just peeked through the stained glass on the side of the door and ran away squealing. They were the first to make it that far tonight."

There was a touch of sadness in her tone, and he thought about all the stories people had told about the "witches who lived on the hill." She must've led such a lonely life after he'd left her.

Another bell chime. He got to his feet. "Persistent buggers. I'll get this. You rest."

With a grateful sigh, Meggie lay back down, tenting her hands over her tummy. He smiled at the sight, then walked toward the foyer, noticing for the first time how she'd set out a bowl of candies. Candlelight flickered from the mouths and eyes of carved pumpkins who sported crooked, tooth-spiked grimaces.

He opened the door and resisted the temptation to act evil and scare the kids. They were at the age when haunted houses shouldn't scare you anymore—maybe fifth grade.

Nick had been scared at that age, of more than ghosts and goblins. He'd been more concerned with his own monsters, ones who wielded razor blades for teeth and skin-burning pokers for fingers.

He cleared his mind, trying to concentrate on how these poor kids stayed back from the door and clutched at their candy bags. They were boys—one Freddy Krueger clone and one X-Man.

"Trick or treat," they mumbled, watching him from beneath lowered masks.

Nick glanced around, noticed how there weren't any more soldiers of bravery in the immediate vicinity and dumped the entire contents of the candy bowl into their bags.

The kids just stared at him.

"Courage rewarded." He shut the door, hearing their whoops of glee and relief as they sprinted from the porch.

Meggie would scold him for getting rid of all the treats, but he didn't intend for them to answer the door anymore tonight. It was late. Anyone who bothered them would probably be out to cause trouble, anyway. He knew that from experience.

When he returned to the living room, he found Meggie fast asleep, a fist tucked against the side of her face. She looked so innocent, so contented. He couldn't help staring for a moment.

What he'd give to touch her beauty.

He leaned down again, coming to one bended knee. He glanced at her flushed face. Out like a light.

Tentatively, hoping not to get caught, he reached out his good hand and laid his fingers on her tummy, closing his eyes, imagining the child inside.

He saw heartbeats, tiny fists clutched to a scrawny chest. "I can't believe you're in there," he said.

He pulled back. Had he just addressed a belly?

Yeah, he had. It felt foolish, but kind of good. The child couldn't pass judgment on him yet. In its eyes, Nick Cassidy was an innocent man.

Heartened, he replaced his touch, cupping her stomach as it rose and fell with the lazy rhythm of sleep. "How're you going to grow up? Huh? Tell me you're going to be just like your mom."

He listened, felt blood flowing through his fingers, felt a slight thud from his own pulse. He didn't really expect an answer, but asking had felt pretty nice.

Meggie stirred, rolling her head so she faced away from him. With a start Nick stood, looking around as guilt heated his skin.

He slipped his arms under her body, gently carrying her to the couch, where he laid her down and tucked a comforter around the curves of her body.

Then, without another glance, he went to his office to try to forget about what he'd just done.

* * *

The next evening Meg closed up the bakery, the bells tinkling as she shut the door behind her and Deacon Chaney. She clutched her deposit bag under an arm beneath her roomy sheepskin coat.

The bakery had been making more profits than ever before. Not that she would've guessed that Nick's return to Kane's Crossing would help business, but in some warped way, it had. More and more citizens had been stopping by for coffee and a snack. More had been lingering in her booths, laughing under the fifties music she liked to play on the new sound system.

She turned around and waved to Nick, who was waiting across the road and leaning against his pickup, leather jacket slumping over flannel and jeans. The bandage had come off of his hand, thank goodness, and he'd gotten that window fixed. She didn't need any more reminders of his flash of temper. Meg thought maybe he'd realized how much his outburst had discomforted her, and had taken great pains to keep his emotions in check.

What a husband, if you could call him that.

She remembered the burn of his hand on her stomach, the amazed glow in his pale gaze, as he'd felt the baby move.

Had she really solved any problems by marrying him? Not really. As expected, she had new things to worry about, things such as ignoring her craving for his touch. She wasn't about to put herself through another heartbreak. Keeping her marriage platonic would help her to avoid that problem.

So then why did her heart yearn for him night after night as she rested in her bed?

Because you're not thinking straight, she thought to

herself. *Be smart, use your brains. Stay away from emotional commitment, since he's not willing to go that far for you.*

He waved back to her, shedding his sunglasses to reveal a smile in his eyes.

She scooted across the street to him, pulling on Deacon's coat so he'd follow. "Nice day at the office?"

"Very productive." He gave the elderly man next to her the once-over and inclined his head toward the empty streets. A hot-pink paper flyer cut through the wind like an aimless wanderer. Green paint-chipped benches rested against walls, as if watching life speed by. Jagged pumpkin shells sprawled over the ground. "This place is a ghost town."

"Spencer High varsity football game. It's the place to be tonight." She went around to her side of the truck and opened the door, tossing in the deposit bag. "Mr. Chaney, do you have a way home?"

The man nodded, his threadbare jacket moving with the accompanying shrug.

Nick slipped his shades back on. "Need a ride?"

Deacon wandered to the truck's hood, inspecting the carbon-clouded red color as if it was a mistake that needed erasing. "Got it covered." He turned his watery gaze on Nick, but something lurked beneath its shallows. Something curious, dark, scary.

He continued. "I suppose you know about the Spencer Market."

Nick just hooked his thumbs through his belt loops. Meg recognized this as a sign of agitation, a protective stance.

"What now?" she asked.

"Rumor has it someone bought it out, just like the

factory. Interesting turn of events recently." Deacon Chaney looked at Nick again.

She agreed, again wondering if Nick had anything to do with the buyouts.

"I remember what it's like to lose a business," said Chaney.

Meg's temper flared. "Nick had nothing to do with the bombing of your shop, Mr. Chaney. Tell him, Nick."

Nick didn't say a word; he just leaned against his truck as if he were having the most pleasant conversation in the world.

Deacon waited a beat, then shook his head. "The Spencers can't be too happy with what's happening, even though there's a passel of people in this town who're clapping their hands behind closed doors."

"What do you mean?" she asked. Meg noticed Nick stiffen slightly, as if newly engaged by the conversation.

"I mean ninety percent of the folks in Kane's Crossing are owned by the Spencers, and our boy Chad is pulling their strings. You can't think they'd be too joyful about that."

Meg shook her head. "That's not true. They love Chad and his family. Just look around you, Mr. Chaney."

Welcome Home banners danced above their heads.

Deacon spread out his arms, back-stepping from the truck. "It's after Halloween, but not everyone has taken off their mask."

And, with that, he sauntered down the street, a grim smile on his whiskered face, the distant sound of football cheers from Spencer Field haunting the air.

Meg threw her hands up and climbed into the truck

cab. Nick followed suit, silent. He doffed his glasses, tucking them into a shirt pocket, then started the engine. It sputtered to life, wheezing like the prophecies of an old, tired man.

"Deacon Chaney needs to watch what he's saying," said Meg, knuckles turning white as she clutched the door handle. "His mouth is going to get him into trouble."

"Why? What's Chad and his protective brood going to do to him that they haven't already done?"

"It's just—" Meg stopped, catching her breath. Getting this riled up might upset the baby. She sighed. "Confrontation isn't the way to go."

Nick was silent for a moment, then, hesitantly, he said, "I recall a girl who never shied away from the right fight. She wouldn't take injustice from anyone."

"That girl was a kid," Meg said, her teeth clenched. It was true that she'd been freer when she was young. She'd flirted, she'd danced over green grass and kicked up water sparkles from the banks of Cutter's Lake. But life changed you, it made you warier, more aware of the price of fighting back. That's why she'd been hiding most of her life behind the walls of a dark, menacing house—to avoid fights and anger. To avoid making more painful memories. After all, look what had happened when she had ventured from behind its walls. She'd messed up with Chad.

Nick reached out to touch her arm. Even through the thick skin of her coat, she could still feel the heat of his fingertips. "I'm sorry, Meggie. I don't mean to upset you. But don't you think *someone* needs to make Chad Spencer and his family pay for what they've done?"

His sentiments stunned her. "What are you saying?"

His hand dropped to the seat, causing a dull thud to echo in her ears. "Nothing. Never mind, Meggie."

"No, I want you to tell me."

They came to a slow stop at a red light on the edge of town, and he thumbed at the faint scars on his hand. "What comes around goes around. Yet, sometimes, fate needs to be hurried along, or else we'll all lose hope."

This was the Nick she knew from their philosophic sessions while stretched out on their backs on a slope of Cutter's Hill. They used to go there to relax, to talk about their futures. In spite of his reticence, he'd always managed to make her pause with his reasoning.

She was almost afraid to ask. "Are you helping something along, Nick?"

"No worries, Meggie. I'm here to help *you*."

Getting information out of him was like trying to pry two extra-strength magnets apart. She dropped the subject for the time being.

When they arrived home, Meg stretched her arms over her head and went to her room to dress into exercise clothing—roomy overalls, a loose long johns shirt, a clip to hold the hair off her neck and cushiony sneakers. For the past couple of nights, Nick had joined her on walks around the hill. She was thankful that he was finally interested in becoming at least a support system for the dreaded hour of exercise each night.

She gently made her way down the steps, noticing that Nick had his back to her.

"Ready to burn up the roads?" she asked.

He turned around, a stiff piece of paper in hand. His eyebrow was cocked, questioning. "Does this belong to you?"

He held up the object. It was a picture, faded colors

of a red corduroy jumper and white turtleneck top dominating her sight until her gaze focused.

Oh, God. That bald little head with wisps of hair. That toothless, slobber-stringed laugh. The round-as-a-lollipop blue eyes laughing out at her.

"Where did you get that?" she asked, breath caught in her chest.

"I was going through the drawers in my office desk. Who is it? Cute little bugger."

She turned her back on him. God help her if he read anything into her expression. "Put it away. Just get it out of my sight."

Silence. Then the clomp of his boots, retreating from her.

Left alone, once again, Meg crumpled to the wooden floor, tears burning her throat as she tried to hold them back.

She couldn't do it.

Meggie had needed some time alone; he could tell by the shrill tone of her voice, the stiff set of her shoulders.

But it'd been enough time.

Nick returned from his foray into the workshop where he'd puttered around by shining up the last of the cradle. It looked damned good, if he said so himself.

He wondered what had been so bad about the picture of the infant. As with many things, it'd just popped up in an unexpected place. He thought maybe it'd been a relative of Meggie's, but he didn't think she had any brothers or sisters.

So why had she turned away from him? Should he have stayed, let her have a shoulder to cry on?

Nick leaned against the house door frame, planning what he could do to get on Meggie's good side again.

Sam probably would've given him solid, brotherly advice. He'd been the one with the girlfriends, the hard-earned, baby-blue Cadillac that had spent many a night parked on an isolated hill with a comely date in the passenger seat.

Too bad Sam had chosen to treat Nick as a non-person after the explosion. Too bad Sam wasn't here now, to mock punch his shoulder and wink at his younger brother, giving him confidence.

Brushing off the too-bad blues, Nick finally decided what to do with his present situation. He'd apologize to Meggie if that's what she wanted. Especially since it'd do no good to have a pregnant, hormonally difficult woman on the rampage.

When he returned to the house, he found her sleeping on an overstuffed couch. Tear stains streaked her face.

Dammit, he should've stayed.

He thought he felt his heart crack as his gaze meandered over her body, all the curves and sways of it. Again, without thinking, he reached out to touch her.

He cupped her belly. "Is she upset? What can we do about that?"

He waited, as if for an answer. Fool.

This was getting to be a very bad habit. He didn't want Meggie to wake up and see him acting all mushy over a baby that wasn't even his.

Nick removed his hand and retreated into his office, shutting the door, separating himself from his wife and her child.

Chapter Eight

Meg had awakened shortly after falling asleep. She'd dreamed that Nick had been here, cuddling, talking to her.

She rubbed her eyes, thinking how desperate her hormones were, then knocked on his office door frame. Nick looked up from what he was doing at his desk.

"Still up for that walk?" she asked. There had to be a sheepish expression on her face; after all, she'd just broken down in front of the man.

And he didn't look all that comfortable himself. Since an explanation of her behavior wouldn't be forthcoming, she decided to do the next best thing.

Blame it on her raging body chemistry. "Sorry about the crying jag. Emotions just overcome me lately, what, with the pregnancy and all. It's played with my body. I never used to sleep this much."

"Don't worry." He stood, silhouetted by the window's peek of a dusky sky.

He grabbed his leather jacket, and they proceeded out the door, down the hill, down the road, in companionable silence. She knew he wanted to ask her what the baby picture meant to her. Darned if she'd tell.

As they strolled past the cemetery, Meg touched his elbow, indicating that she wanted to take a crooked dirt path that twisted into a copse of pine. "I want to see if you remember this."

Shortly they arrived at a splintered wooden fence, the trees beyond blocking whatever lay behind them. A metal-plate landmarker indicated that this was a historical site of significance. A chain binding the entry fence signaled something more ominous.

"The Meeting House," said Nick, grinning.

Meg returned his smile. Years ago they'd explored this place, only once, at night, and they'd never been back. As always, she'd trusted him to protect her from anything, and that image rang true right now. He seemed so strong and self-assured, even dashing in those holey jeans.

Nick inspected the chain lock. "I wonder if that caretaker is still around. Remember how everyone used to say that he had only one eye and carried around a shotgun?"

"Nobody really sneaks in here anymore. I think everyone has forgotten."

"Funny how the people of Kane's Crossing have selective memories," said Nick. He wedged open the gate, leaving a space large enough to accommodate a wide woman. "Are we going in?"

God, she hadn't felt this daring since they were kids. "You don't mind being chased by the evil caretaker?"

"You're stalling."

She shot him a sidelong glance and squeaked through the opening, followed by Nick. The gate clamped shut with a clang.

He took her hand in his, her fingers digging into his warmth, and they climbed the slight hill to the Meeting House.

It had been constructed during the early 1800s. Supposedly, poor farmers had gathered here to worship and meet socially, but certain tragedies had befallen them, consequently closing the house to anyone ever since. One story had it that star-crossed lovers had been murdered in the house, and their spirits haunted it even to this day.

Meg took a moment to appreciate its stark simplicity—the hand-shaped mud bricks and steeple-roofed splendor. A graveyard with thin, leaning wooden crosses napped next to the house, overshadowed by the white of the larger cemetery next door.

Night was relaxing over the horizon, giving Meg a shiver of trepidation. Why had she brought Nick here anyway? To show him that he'd been wrong this afternoon when he'd accused her of losing her spirit?

A massive pop sounded behind the house. Nick gently pulled her away, toward the hill leading to the gate.

"What're you doing?" she asked. "That was probably just a car on the road."

"Or it could've been the caretaker." He wiggled his eyebrows. "At any rate, I don't want you in danger. Let's go."

Was he kidding? She hadn't felt this unfettered since

she was twelve years old, poking around forbidden places with her summer-time friend.

When exactly had she lost her lust for life? Her sense of adventure? Hiding in her home had become much too easy. What if she could bring herself to take another chance, to live life as a participant, not an observer?

Yeah, you did a great job of participating in Chad's games, said a voice in her head. *See what participating gets you? A big belly and a husband who has no interest in anything but business.*

That wasn't true. Her life was the best it'd been since leaving San Diego.

She turned to Nick, standing on tiptoe to cover his eyes. He jerked back a little, making her regret the impulsive advance.

Darn it, she wouldn't go back into her shell.

She kept her hands where they were. In a soft voice, she said, "Just listen to the sounds, Nick."

The stir of a restless wind blowing over dry pine needles mingled with the stillness of a starry night. The music reminded her of their childhood, of lazy evening preludes to I-don't-have-to-be-anywhere tomorrows.

"Doesn't it take you away?" she asked, her hands slipping from his eyes to land quietly on his broad shoulders.

Maybe her experimental gaiety had gone too far. Nick touched one of her hands, bending his mouth to the skin, rubbing until his five-o'clock shadow whispered against her. He closed his eyes.

A thrill ran down her arm, as light as a palm grazing over tall blades of grass. This was dumb of her, very dumb. "Nick…"

"I know," he said. But instead of putting the brakes

on the situation, he accelerated, taking her index finger between his lips and his teeth, kissing it, teasing the tip.

Meg had always liked the human touch. She'd been an affectionate girl, cuddling in people's laps, hugging friends and relatives. She hadn't been truly held by a man in so long, she thought she'd fade from want of it.

Unable to help herself, she nestled against his firm chest, between the folds of his jacket, enveloping herself in his male scent. She felt her hair scratching his chin, and she could imagine how it caressed the cleft there. The thought gave her a tiny chill of desire.

"Oh, Meggie, I'd always wondered what it'd be like to kiss you."

His body was hard, and she burrowed against it, feeling sinew and the long length of him. She tilted up her chin, seeking his gaze, his lips.

What she saw in his eyes frightened and excited her, causing a shot of longing to bolt through her stomach. She wondered if the baby could feel it, if it was inappropriate to subject him or her to such hunger.

When his heated mouth settled over hers, she forgot everything. There was only Nick, his lips demanding a response from her. She threaded her fingers through his need-a-trim hair, marveling at how soft it was, loving the boyish way it curled at the ends.

The wedding kiss had only been a hint of his desire; a hard bulge in his jeans indicated the extent of it now. Meg sucked in a breath in reaction to the pounding of her heartbeat, then joined her mouth with his once again.

The night wrapped around them, pulling their bodies closer together. He ran his hands over her arms, upward, thumbs skimming the throbbing veins in her neck.

Her pulse crashed against his touch, beating like running footsteps. And half of her did want to back away, preserving her emotions. But half of her wanted more, wanted him to brush her clothes off her body, wanted him to whisper promises that would no doubt fade with the sunset.

As his tongue warmed hers, Meg pressed closer to him, almost losing herself in this dream that would never amount to anything more than a kiss in the woods. If she valued her well-being, she'd stop this breathless anticipation of what his hands would cup next, this longing for Nick to at least care for her.

He moved his fingers down her throat, over her collarbone, leaving a boneless heat that spread all over her body, moving in time to the night sounds. The pressure of his mouth became more demanding as his fingertips skimmed over the swell of her breasts.

She stepped back, restless, afraid, almost clawing for breath.

He sighed deeply, running a hand through his hair. "Sorry about that."

Sorry? She managed a tight laugh. Sorry that he'd kissed her? Sorry that she'd almost given in to her body's wish list?

"No worries, Nick," she mumbled, trying to lighten the moment. She was sorry, too, for thinking the kiss might've meant something to him.

They stood for a moment, listening to those same evening songs, pines casting ever-long shadows over their faces, like fingers creeping toward their throats.

He shuffled his booted feet, cleared his throat. "I suppose it's time to leave."

"I suppose." She glanced at a wooden cross marking a farmer's final resting place, wondering if she'd bury her newfound hope there when she left.

He nodded, back to being the kid who never wasted a word unless forced to. Well, she wasn't about to strong-arm anything from him.

They walked down the hill, the space between them as deep as a freshly turned grave.

A couple of days later Nick was still reeling with the implications of that kiss.

He wasn't sure when his body had crossed the line from sane to runaway train. Had it been when he'd grabbed Meggie's hand to walk up that hill? Or maybe he'd lost control when she'd touched him, covering his eyes, making him imagine that they were in a room with a comfortable place to lay her down and kiss the length of her body.

Whatever the reason, he'd gone too far. His hands had developed a mind of their own, wanting to touch more than her face or her throat. They'd wanted to travel the course of her swollen breasts, the curve of her backside.

But Meggie had stepped back, evidently wanting no more than a cuddle. But hadn't she responded to him just as passionately as he'd hoped?

It was just as well she'd pulled back, because Nick wasn't so sure he was comfortable himself with intimacy.

When he'd kissed her, it had felt as if he'd stepped into a velvet-lined trap—seductive, yet lethal. Was he prepared to be part of her family? Not merely a figurehead husband, but one in every sense of the word?

All his life he'd made a career of being kicked out

of families. He wasn't sure he knew how to be a part of one, especially one that featured a kid he hadn't even fathered.

Too late now. He'd married into a family situation, but that didn't mean he had to fully invest himself emotionally. He'd aid Meggie while she needed it most, then go on with his life when she didn't require his help anymore. It was the fair thing to do for her. She'd never asked for anything more.

In the meantime he didn't want Meggie to shy away from him, to be afraid that he'd try to take advantage of their marriage again.

So he'd made an attempt to assuage his guilt. He'd taken her shopping for baby stuff.

Here they were, in the middle of the Mercantile Department Store's infant section, surrounded by a pastel wonderland of terry-cloth sleepers, hardy diaper bags and fluffy receiving blankets. Baby powder aromas lingered on the air as the store speakers plied them with a Muzak rendition of "Twinkle, Twinkle Little Star." As he read the merchandise labels, he shook his head with the thought of how much care a child required.

Meggie stopped her inspection of a bedding set and turned her attention to him. "Are you still sore because I dragged you into this place?"

"I'm here under protest." But he wouldn't fight her when it came to choice of shopping venue. Besides, Nick was curious about the department store he'd soon own. Yeah, things were going well with his financial plan. Tomorrow the final details for the Spencers' hardware store would be completed, and the town would whisper some more about the mysterious new owner. And, most importantly of all, his college buddy had almost finalized the Spencer Bank takeover.

He could hardly wait.

Two girls at the sales counter giggled as they murmured to each other. They peeked at him, then tittered once more.

Nick tried to ignore them. He fingered a sea-green bib that had "Daddy's Little Girl" scrawled in cursive threading across it. Another round of guilt assaulted him. He wondered if he'd even get to see the child grow from cradle to crib.

Meggie wandered closer to the counter, seemingly oblivious to the gossiping salesclerks. He shadowed her, ready to glare at anyone who dared toss an insult her way.

A lace-fringed bassinet stood on a raised display pedestal. Meggie halted in her tracks, her eyes wide. "That's beautiful."

Nick thought of the cradle he'd restored at home. "Maybe we should hold off on that for now."

"Of course." She took one last look at it, then moved on to a rattle and bottle shelf.

He didn't have to remind her that money was no object; she could buy whatever her heart desired for the child. Did she think it strange that he'd turned her away from the bassinet?

They'd moved so close to the salesgirls that he could clearly hear their topic. With a sense of relief, he heard other names being bandied about. He was so used to being the target of insults lately that he half expected to be the subject of the present conversation.

As he picked up a layette gown—that's what the label said, at least—he heard a name that perked up his ears.

"Did you hear about Chad in Europe?"

The other girl, "Mmmed" as if tasting a good bit of chocolate. "No. What's happening there?"

Nick braved a glance at Meggie, whose cheeks had flushed. He noticed that she'd moved a little closer to the counter, poking at a rack full of bear, bunny and duck-laden sleepers.

The gossip continued. "I hear tell that Chad's engaged!"

"No!"

"Yes."

A long pause stretched the tension. Nick wondered if hearts were breaking all over Kane's Crossing at this news.

"Well," continued one girl, "they say she's lovely, rich...but—"

"What?"

A forceful whisper. "She can't have kids. Barren as an arctic ice floe."

"Matilda, you shouldn't say such things."

Nick realized he was too close, that he'd probably find out more information by relocating to a more discreet spot. He pretended to be enamored of a rocking chair, testing the wood after he bent among the clothing racks. Even though Meggie was near the conversation, the clerks didn't seem to mind her presence.

"Macy, I'll say anything I please. Anyway, that's the scuttlebutt. I can't wait until he gets home."

Their idle talk drifted to other names, other scandals, but Nick tuned out their chatter. He had enough to assimilate.

What exactly did this news mean to him and Meggie?

A fire burned bright in his belly, the fire of revenge. If this gossip was true, it upped the stakes for Chad's downfall. What would happen if Spencer's fiancée found out that he'd fathered a child by another woman? Would she bloody his heart to a black pulp, leaving him broken and burned?

Or would they go after Meggie's child?

On one hand, Nick could picture the expression on Spencer's face when his intended dumped him. Beaten, put in his place. Maybe he was even marrying her for money, in light of his family's recent misfortunes with their businesses.

But what would happen to Meggie if they wanted her child? If the rumor of a barren bride was true, then chances were good that they'd eventually want Chad's own son or daughter to raise.

He cleared his mind of such thoughts. Even if he was burning to do so, revealing Meggie's secret to Chad couldn't be an option. Not anymore.

Fleeting images of smoke, ashes and fire assailed Nick.

Justice.

No, by God. Could he stoop low enough to tell Chad's fiancée that her future groom had neglected his duty to another woman? Even if Spencer deserved the consequences?

What if he could hide Meggie in that dream house with her child, making sure Spencer never found them to claim the baby? What if Nick could have the pleasure of telling Chad the news, face-to-face, exploding a bomb of a different sort into Chad's existence? It'd feel damn satisfying to rub the golden boy's nose in his mistakes.

Once again, guilt made him pause. What would happen to Meggie after Spencer realized that Nick had married the mother of his child?

He ran his hand over the rocking chair, standing as he went.

Someday, Meggie would coax her baby to sleep in this contraption. She'd hold the child close to her heart, nursing him or her, singing soft lullabies that would float through the house like magnolia perfume. He'd never see the baby close his or her eyes in slumber, all innocence and light, all the things he wasn't.

He'd never get to see mother and child cradled together if he exacted revenge in this way.

Across a sea of infant products, Meggie trudged between the racks, rubbing her arms. She'd heard the salesclerks, and the gossip had worried her. That was obvious.

Now what was he going to do to make her feel better?

Pinks, blues, greens, yellows... The colors swirled in a vortex in front of Meg's vision, sucking her into a shocked silence.

It wasn't the news of the engagement that'd stunned her. It was the second part—the part about Chad's bride not being able to have her own babies.

Now, Kane's Crossing gossip had never been high on her list of accurate sources. It ranked right up there with tabloid magazines and the county newspaper. But Meg knew in her heart that she needed to be prepared for the worst when Chad returned home; she needed to be able to fight for her child, no matter the situation.

What would she do if Chad's wife wanted her baby?

One thing was for sure—she'd never let that happen. Hadn't she married Nick for that reason? As a preventive plan, to secure the belief that he'd fathered the baby?

Maybe she should run away, as Nick had suggested when he'd first gotten into town. But running away meant leaving a haunted past behind, always being afraid, always having to peek around corners to make sure Chad wasn't waiting there for her and her child. She'd been running for too long and, frankly, she was sick to death of it.

She was ready to face Chad. Maybe.

Damn this lack of confidence. Damn this town. Damn her inability to make up her mind.

Nick's boot steps thumped behind her and she turned to peer up at him. As always, his torn-jeans attitude jerked her heart to attention.

"I'm not in a shopping mood today," she said.

He guided her out of the store, his hand on her back, reassuring and strong. This was the man who'd saved her baby. She'd be eternally grateful.

Neither of them mentioned the gossip, and Meg took that as a good sign.

She never paused to reflect on the cold, hungry set of his jaw or the dead-steel glint of his eyes.

Chapter Nine

Through the haze of a daydream, Rachel Shane drifted into Meg's view, accompanied by the realization that her cinnamon toast was probably more than well done.

"Ah, Meg? Hello in there?"

Meg blinked, squinting her eyes as her friend and the bakery's back room came into focus. It was official—her quiet time was over.

She'd been obsessing about yesterday's news regarding Chad's engagement, and how it'd affect her new family's life. No easy solutions had presented themselves during her moment of mental escape. Had she really expected answers?

It was Rachel's day off from the hospital, and she'd hired a baby-sitter to watch her young daughter on the horse farm while she helped Meg in the bakery. Presently, they were whipping up a batch of chocolate-chip cookies.

Rachel's gray-green eyes shone with laughter as she went back to sprinkling chocolate morsels into a bowl of lumpy batter. "What I'd give to be a visitor in your brain. Or maybe not. There'd be 'Twilight Zone' signposts all over the place, I'll bet."

Meg pushed away from the counter, dusting flour from her hands. She donned an oven mitt and took the toast out of the oven. "You don't know the half of it," she said, images of Nick crashing through her thoughts.

"I didn't think anyone in this speck of a town had anything to think about other than football and gossip."

A never-ending circle, leading right back to Meg's thoughts. She wouldn't waste their time talking about Chad with Rachel.

Her friend was still dealing with the disappearance of her husband. "Any news about Matthew?"

Tough to the end, Rachel beat the batter a little harder, avoiding Meg's gaze. A strand of shoulder-length ash-brown hair fell into her eyes from the confines of its barrette. "My money-gouging detective says that Matthew's trail leads to Louisiana, but it ends there. Zip—just like that." Her voice broke on the last word.

Damn Matthew Shane. She wouldn't be surprised if he was painting some other town red while forgetting about his wife and five-year-old daughter at home. He'd been that way ever since they were young, and she'd wanted to knock some sense into him then, as well.

"I know I keep saying this, but things will turn out okay."

"Like it did for you." Rachel wiped the wooden spoon on the side of the bowl. "It's a good thing Nick

Cassidy came back to marry you and claim the baby. But, all the same, I still don't trust the guy.''

Meg wished her friend had the same confidence when it came to trusting Rachel's own husband. "Nick's a good man, Rachel. You can meet him when he picks me up.''

"I've seen your good man strutting around town in that mystery-guy getup. Nobody seems to know much about him, except for his fantastic bomb squad performance.'' Rachel shrugged. "I just don't know if I like him, even if he is your spouse.''

Meg was about to point out that Rachel didn't exactly corner the market on trust at the present time. How could she, with a husband who might've run off and deserted her?

"Nick's nothing like other men.'' Meg felt her body go soft, tingling with joy. "He's decent, honest and very much a person of honor.''

Rachel's hand froze in midair, a ball of dough between her fingers, as she watched Meg wax eloquent about Nick. "You seem to be very much in love with your business-arrangement hubby, Meg.''

Her? Maybe lust was part of the equation, but... love?

Meg laughed. "I think you're jumping the gun.''

"I'm not hitting that far off the mark. Am I?''

Meg fanned herself, pretending to not have heard the last remark. "I need to get to the counter to wait on my customers.''

"Top priority,'' was the sarcastic comeback.

Meg grinned as she used her backside to push through the double door. "It's usually slow around closing time. Don't give me grief.''

To her surprise, Nick had already arrived at the bakery to drive her home. And he was sitting with Deacon Chaney at the old man's regular booth.

It'd been rare to get a smile out of him since yesterday. As she walked to their seats, she wondered if the salesclerks' gossip had put a damper on his mood.

Why couldn't he just forget about Chad?

Then again, how could he, with this child and with the way Chad had shaped Nick's life?

"My favorite customers," she said, gesturing to the near-empty stillness of late afternoon.

Deacon Chaney stared at her stomach. "She *is* big."

Protectively, Meg's hands sought her belly. From the books she'd read, she knew she was larger than normal at this time in her pregnancy, but his comment was really sort of rude.

Chaney continued, this time addressing Nick. "I think you're right about her not working here for a while."

She pointed and tapped a finger on the table in front of her husband. "Is this everyone's business?"

Nick sat back against the vinyl upholstery, a smile barely tipping his mouth. The mouth she'd kissed just days ago. What she'd give to feel it again.

Obviously an answer wasn't in the cards for him. Back to strong and silent.

Chaney said, "Two more stubborn people I've never seen. A mule-headed baker and her secret-hoarding husband." His conversation abruptly switched gears. "Say, you heard about the hardware store, Nick?"

A lift of Nick's brows was the only response.

"Ah, this is going nowhere." Deacon slipped out of the booth, tipped his head to Meg and left the bakery.

"Now the Spencer hardware store has taken a dive, hmm?" she asked. When he didn't answer, Meg took

Deacon's place in the booth, sighing as she relieved her feet of the extra weight, sighing because he didn't often lose control of his poker face.

She changed the subject, almost out of desperation to get a reaction out of him. "I won't stop working. This bakery was Aunt Valentine's pride and joy, and I mean to keep it alive."

"It won't bring her back."

In spite of her success at drawing him out, she glared at him. "I know that."

"I'm not sure you do, Meggie. When are you going to do what's best for yourself?"

Anger tinged his low tone, and she wondered what she'd done to earn his ire. "If you've had a bad day, don't take it out on me."

In apparent frustration, he ran a hand over his stubble, the friction making her shiver with a yearning so strong it stung.

"I don't mean to sound cross," he said. "But—"

He glanced over Meg's shoulder.

Rachel walked into the room, untying her apron as she went along. "But what, Mr. Cassidy? Why don't you aim your foul mood at somebody less vulnerable?"

His shoulders sunk, as if saying, "Not another problem."

Meg wasn't sure how to handle the situation, so she did what first came to mind. "Rachel Shane, this is my husband, Nick."

Rachel crossed her arms. Nick stared right back.

Wonderful, thought Meg. Another bakery showdown.

"You know what?" she said, trying to gracefully ease herself out of the booth. "This is too intense for me. If you two want to duel it out, be my guests. Rachel, just make sure you close up shop. Nick, I'll see you at home."

"Wait," they both said in unison.

Nick stood and extended his hand to Rachel. "Pleased to meet you, Ms. Shane."

"Likewise." She widened her eyes at Meg. He hooked his thumbs in his belt loops. *Satisfied?*

Meg knew a smug smile lingered on her face. "That's a good start. Now maybe you both will mean it when you meet the next time."

Rachel marched past her into the back room without another thought to Nick. "I'll finish these cookies and lock up."

"Take them home with the cinnamon toast," said Meg. "I'll blow up even more if I eat them."

Nick sent a longing gaze to the back room, then the expression passed.

Well, if he wanted cookies and sweet toast, he could overcome his silent habits and ask for them, thought Meg.

Cranky girl. She needed another nap.

"Thanks, Rachel," she yelled, then walked past Nick, out the front door, noticing his slightly wounded expression as she'd passed.

Guilt, heavy as rain clouds. She decided to wait for him to catch up with her, noticing that the sky was an angry gray, the air carrying the smell of sulfur.

She hoped the night wouldn't be as stormy as her present attitude.

Dinner was tense, the promise of disagreement hanging in the air above them.

After eating, Meg watched Nick go to his office to

work. She decided she'd exercise by herself tonight. Obviously, they needed time away from each other.

Meg grinned to herself. Right. If that was true, why did the world seem a little less colorful without him in it?

She changed into tennis shoes and gray sweats, stopping briefly to twist her curls into a lopsided bun. Then she stepped quietly through the kitchen door into the backyard.

In the distance, thunder rumbled, reflecting her mood. The wind chopped against her, rustling branches of the apple tree near the garden.

She stopped. Maybe a walk was out of the question. But returning to the house sure wasn't an option; she'd suffocate from tension unless she loosened her muscles and filled her lungs with herb-tinged air.

The workshop shed stood to the side, its clapboard walls dotted by two darkened windows. She hadn't gone inside since Aunt Valentine had passed away. It was silly, really. Her aunt used to mix perfumes in the workshop. The kids in town always said that the old witch was mixing brews, but Meg knew better.

She peeked back at the storm clouds, the cotton-ball puffs growing sootier by the minute.

Exploring would be fun, distracting her from her crabbiness. She ducked inside the shop door, feeling for the switch leading to the tin-shelled light bulb that dangled from the ceiling.

A weak, butter-hued light suffused the small room, melting over plastic-shrouded furniture, beakers and Bunsen burners scattered over the work counter. A vintage Harley hid in a corner. Meg leaned back her head, inhaling the hint of distilled flowers and spice.

The thunder spoke again, louder this time.

Something out of place caught her eye. It was nestled between a tarped armoire and a bundle of damask curtains. When she crept closer to take a look, she discovered that the object was a cradle.

Smoothing her fingers down the hood, she realized that the piece had been recently refurbished; the woodsy, head-spinning scent of varnish seeped from the strands of wicker. When she peeked inside, she "Aa-ahed" at the new fabric—yellow and spring-leaf green kittens pawing at balls of yarn.

Had Nick done this?

Her heart lodged in her throat, encouraging tears of happiness and frustration. He'd never said outright that he loved the baby. Sure, he'd touched her stomach a time or two, but she thought maybe he'd merely been curious.

But this...this was an act of patience, of caring.

Did he feel more for her and her child than he admitted?

No, she wouldn't allow herself to hope. Expecting more than a business marriage from Nick was foolish. He'd been more than gracious to offer his name to her. She shouldn't pressure him—or herself—to become a real family. After all, he hadn't signed on for real daddy duty.

A heady magnolia fragrance clouded around her head, making Meg feel sleepy. Forget the walk for tonight, she told herself. The baby needed rest. Her *mind* needed rest.

Meg followed the perfume back to the house, where she'd have to walk past Nick's office.

Nick heard the kitchen door flop against the frame. He turned off his office desk light and leaned back in his stuffed swivel chair.

He'd only go out there to talk with Meggie if they didn't argue. Their disagreements about her bakery work and his unwillingness to tell her about his business takeover plan for the Spencers couldn't be good for the baby's health. That's one of the reasons he stayed silent most of the time—because he didn't want Meggie to know more than she needed to. If she knew what he was doing to the Spencer family, she'd go ballistic for certain.

That's right, Meggie didn't condone his anger, and part of Nick couldn't blame her.

But the other part cheered it full-force. There wasn't a night that went by when he hadn't bolted up in bed with the word "justice" reverberating through the room, echoing in time to the bass-drum beat of his heart. Every bead of nightmare sweat on his skin was another reason to give Chad Spencer his due.

Soft footsteps brushed against the hallway carpet, covered only by a slap of thunder. It shook the walls with its nearness, driving discomfort through him like a nail through wood.

He'd always hated storms, ever since he could remember. One of his first memories had been from the viewpoint of a child huddled under a table, cowering from thunder as mighty as a scream, lightning as blinding as a flying fist.

Meggie peered around the door frame, her features lit by a flash. She smiled at him shyly, opened her mouth to say something. Then she snapped her lips shut.

He tried to grin, too. "Scared of storms?"

He unwrapped his fingers from the arms of the chair,

only now realizing that he'd been clutching the furniture. He stood, just as thunder crashed again. Dammit, he didn't want Meggie to see what this storm was doing to him.

Meggie shook her head, making the curls that had escaped from the bun in her hair spring up and down. "Actually, I enjoy watching rainstorms." She frowned at him. "We hid in a cave once when we were young, watching the rain. Remember? I was pretty brave *then*."

She sure had been. However, he, himself, wasn't afraid of a little rain. It was the rest of the package that got to him. "That shower wasn't a showcase for an electricity explosion, like this one."

"Come with me." She held out her hand to him.

His pulse pounded double time in accord with his footsteps. When their hands touched, it seemed as if the lightning had found his skin, sizzling and tingling.

She led him to the front porch, where a wooden slide-swing waited. They cuddled back against the wide, cool pillows and watched as the rain began to fall. He rested his arm on the top of the swing, trying to relax.

As if on cue, Meggie settled into the crook of his arm, her head nuzzled against his chin. Without thinking, he placed his other hand on her stomach.

Thunder again, quaking his body. Lightning on its tail, chasing the storm.

He spidered his fingers, feeling movement in her belly. Then he smiled, almost forgetting about the elements.

An unborn child had no guilt. It couldn't choose its parents, couldn't choose its lot in life.

Nick wondered why some children were lucky

enough to get a mom like Meggie, and why some were fated to foster homes and juvenile hall.

He'd started out innocent, but it seemed that he'd lost it upon entering the world. His life had gotten worse until someone had slammed him to rock bottom. Someone who would be hitting the depths of despair, himself, if Nick had anything to do with it.

As Nick breathed in Meggie's fruit-washed scent, he closed his eyes, lost in the thunder, almost wishing he could allow *this* someone to help chase his demons away.

The sway of the swing mingled with the cool freshness of rain to make Meggie sleepy, putting ridiculous thoughts into her head, thoughts along the lines of what it would be like if Nick loved her.

It wasn't the first time she'd imagined the scenario. Long ago, at Cutter's Hill, she'd thought about the same sentiment. It'd been the day Nick was run out of town, and they'd been hiding from Chad Spencer that afternoon.

She recalled resting her head against his chest, flapping her eyelashes to test the strength of her preteen-queen charm. Then she'd asked him, "Do you love me, Nick?" or something equally foolish.

The expression on his face had clammed her up, had made her want to crawl into the rocks of their hiding place and never come out. Naturally he'd told her that he didn't love her, and, really, she hadn't been too surprised. She wasn't even sure why she'd even asked in the first place.

One thing was certain. She'd never ask that question again. The answer had stung too much, and she didn't need an instant replay of the mortification.

As they glided back and forth on the carved wooden swing, Meg felt the urge to move away from Nick, to preserve her heart from another whipping. But the touch of his hand on her baby's little dwelling gave her pause.

Would he be touching her like this if she hadn't gotten pregnant?

Don't even think about it, she thought. You need to feel good about yourself, because a happy mother is a healthy mother.

Thunder rocked the skies again, growing fainter as the storm passed. Nick's muscles bunched under his flannel shirt.

She'd noticed his barely controlled agitation when he'd stood in his office, but she hadn't thought much of it. Nick was always brave, always the one who sheltered her. Meg didn't think he was afraid of anything.

He'd always been her protector.

Maybe she could help him relax, distract him from the violence of the weather. "Did you have a good day at work?"

His firm biceps tensed again. So much for relaxation. "Sure."

Terse. She couldn't describe him with any other words. Was there any way to convince him to share a part of his life with her, something more than just a fake marriage?

She sighed without really meaning to. "I wish we could be honest with each other."

Images of Nick showing her the baby picture clouded her mind. She was nothing but a hypocrite if *she* wasn't willing to expose her secrets, as well.

His silence gathered, then dissipated. "Me, too, Meggie."

The far-off grumble of the storm covered the dead air.

She wanted to ask him everything. About life after he'd been kicked out of Kane's Crossing, about all the businesses that had been mysteriously purchased since his return and, most importantly, about the haunted shadow that lurked in his pale eyes.

Darn it, she was going to throw caution to the calming wind. Meg shifted in her seat, looking up at him. "Nick, you've been telling me that you're in town to protect people from Chad. Is there something more to it than that?"

He avoided her searching gaze. His response was a long time in coming. "There's much more to it, Meggie, but I don't care to talk about it."

She gave up trying to make eye contact and leaned her head back on his shoulder. "I don't guess I should be shocked."

His chest rose with a harsh chuckle. "I'm not worth your concern. Just know that I'll be here for you. Our deal didn't include the exchange of vital statistics."

"Evidently not."

God, she hated to sound bitter, but his reticence was driving her nuts.

His hands left her shoulder and stomach in a careless gesture of surrender. He spread out his fingers, as if to say, "Bring it on."

"You want to know why I'm here?"

"Yes."

He rested his hands on her again, causing the inside of her stomach to flutter a time or two. "Besides what I've already told you about finding my foster family and making sure Chad never hurts anyone again…"

He trailed off. Meg wasn't even sure he'd continue,

but, when he did, his low, gravely voice held a note of resignation.

"Months ago, I almost died. I was driving home with a 'friend'—" his tone placed invisible quotation marks around the last word "—when we crashed head-on into a streetlight. She was uninjured by some miracle, but I vegetated in a hospital until I was fit to leave."

He stopped the swing from moving with a scrape of his boots. "Death puts things in their place. It makes you see the world in a different light. The split second after I had that car wrapped around my body, I saw everything through a sheet of blood. And I realized that I needed to come back to Kane's Crossing to take care of things." He shrugged. "I'm doing just that. Who knows how much more time I have."

Meg swallowed, coating her dry throat with courage.

She'd married a dark angel who'd come back from the brink of death with something more than a pleasant trip to his childhood home in mind.

The question was, what was his plan, and how did she and her unborn child fit into it?

Chapter Ten

As it happened, Meg never got an answer from Nick regarding his plan for Kane's Crossing. In fact, she never even asked.

The groan of the swing's sliding mechanism had covered their awkward silence, and, finally, they'd gone inside. Each to their own rooms.

For the next week they'd gone about their business without approaching another upsetting conversation. Meg was almost afraid to ask him more about his life; what he'd revealed already was jarring enough. Yet she wanted to know everything about him, wanted to reach out a soothing hand to calm his troubles.

Right, as if he'd reveal more about himself than he needed to. She should just be grateful for what he'd done for her already and not demand anything more from him.

One sunny day, after arriving home from an extremely slow day at work, Meg changed into comfortable clothes and sprawled out on the overstuffed sofa in the parlor, the late-afternoon light from the bay window brightening the cream wall paint to a relaxing shade. She'd snatched the daily paper from the kitchen table, where Nick had spread it after he'd picked her up from the bakery. He'd read it for a short time, then closed himself up in his office.

Heck, she'd read this rag for pure entertainment. The journalistic quality wasn't much better than the rantings of a brain-addled parrot, as far as she was concerned.

She scanned the front page, widening her eyes as the headline screamed the urgent news: Mercantile And Bank Drop Out Of Spencers' Hands!

Her heart lunged. Both properties, sold to a mystery buyer. Why hadn't she heard anything about this today? She wondered if Nick had left this paper out on purpose. It wasn't like him to trail a mess around the house.

Unable to stop herself, she kept reading, mumbling as she sped along. "'Mercantile Department Store and Spencer's Bank...jewels in the crown of Spencer holdings...family left only with Perky Puppy Grooming Salon...Deacon Chaney...'"

She stopped, her eyes moving a bit more slowly at this sentence. "'Deacon Chaney has taken ownership of the Mercantile.'"

The paper drifted out of her hands to the sofa. What? Was Mr. Chaney the one who'd been buying all the Spencer property? It didn't make sense, because the elderly man had been left nearly destitute after his drugstore had been bombed. He'd been living off the kindness of his son, as a matter of fact.

Meg thought of Nick's office, all the equipment.

She grabbed the paper again and hurried to his door. After she knocked, a muffled, "Come in" convinced her to enter.

The door cackled on its hinges as it opened. Nick was reclining in his black leather office chair, staring at a computer monitor, boots propped up on the cherrywood desk, flannel shirt opened to reveal a worn T-shirt. Meg could faintly see the outline of his muscled chest beneath the thin, white material. The sight shortened her breath.

"I, uh…" She sighed, shoving the newspaper's front page into his line of vision. Her question stayed strangled at the back of her throat as he straightened in his seat.

"Oh, that," he said, a satisfied grin on his face.

What was he so chipper about? Of course, "chipper" was far too strong a word to describe his mood, but it was all relative.

"I almost tripped over the headline," she said. "Is there something you want to tell me?"

"I just thought you'd want to know."

She wasn't about to go around this frustrating verbal circle again. When he felt like opening up to her, she'd listen, but she wasn't going to agonize over his inability to share his life with her. It wasn't even her right to expect it. "Okay, Nick. I'm going for my walk."

His head snapped up from some paperwork he was inspecting. "Can I finish this up and go with you?"

Meg almost lost her balance when she detected a note of enthusiasm in his low voice. "Sure," she said. "I'll be in the parlor."

His lips curved up at the corners. Meg tried her own weak smile, but surrendered it when Nick immersed himself in his work once again. She folded the paper and placed it on the end table near the door, then walked to the parlor, where she snuggled onto her favorite napping spot in the house—the welcoming overstuffed sofa.

Thoughts of Nick swirled around her brain like the mingling of oil and water. She couldn't begin to reconcile the different sides of him. On one hand, he was kind and protective, just like the boy she'd known. On the other, he was mysterious, with dark undercurrents of controlled violence. How could one man contain all these emotions and stay sane?

Maybe she was just *in*sane for marrying him, someone who was little more than a stranger, even after weeks of matrimonial "bliss."

She must've drifted off to sleep, as was normal for her this time of day. Because the next thing she knew, she was dreaming about Nick's low-thunder voice, Nick's large, strong hand over the curve of the baby in her body.

Slowly, she opened her eyes, her heart exploding as she realized it wasn't a dream. Nick was here, bent over her stomach, talking to the air...talking to her unborn child.

"Do you sleep when your mom sleeps?" he asked, his thumb rubbing circles over her skin, warming areas that should've been left dormant when Chad disappeared.

She laughed, jarring Nick from his conversation. He rose to his feet, all power and embarrassment, his towering height made less intimidating by the boyish ruddiness creeping up his neck.

His thumbs found their way into the belt loops. "Ready to go?"

The temptation to comment on his baby talk was

overwhelming, yet she couldn't bring herself to heighten the mortification staining his face. "Ready." She almost added, "Daddy," but knew she was jumping to conclusions.

The cradle in the workshop. The way he touched her stomach. The smooth wonder in his voice as he conversed with the baby. Would it be wrong to think that Nick was warming up to Chad's child?

She thought of all the businesses being taken over around town. Maybe it would be a false assumption. After all, he hadn't come back to Kane's Crossing for her.

He'd returned for reasons more unfathomable than the darkest part of the ocean. Reasons that made her shiver from the chill.

She tried her best to smile. "Ready when you are."

Nick felt like an idiot. He'd packed a cooler full of food for a light picnic, hoping to drive Meggie away from questions about the Mercantile, the bank, the market, the hardware store....

He should've known she'd ask him about the news headline, and part of Nick wanted to tell her all about his plan for Spencer justice. But another part wanted to protect her from his darkness, from any ugliness this world had to offer.

They'd strolled to Cutter's Hill and, while Meggie spread out a blanket so they could view the lake with its glimmer of sunset-colored wedges on the choppy water, he unpacked the cooler. Milk for Meggie, strawberries and oranges, spinach quiche, whole-grain muffins, pumpkin bread and baked Cornish hens. He'd gone to the market today—*his* market now—to secure a proper dinner for her. If she insisted on working, the least he could do was make sure she ate decently.

They reclined on the hill, leaning into the slope of it, hearing the dried grass crunch against the blanket. Meggie unclipped her hair, allowing the burnished curls to spring free. If Nick had been the smooth Chad Spencer type, he would've told her that the color of her hair reminded him of the fiery sky.

But what good did pretty words do? He wanted no part of Spencer, anyway. Even all these material things that came with owning millions of dollars didn't impress Nick. The Spencer family lived for status symbols—fancy houses, sleek cars with shining chrome and sparkling paint jobs. Nick preferred a road-hammered pickup and comfortable blue jeans. The only time he'd given in to a taste for the material was when he'd purchased Meggie's wedding ring. It matched the shine of her eyes.

Besides, he'd spend any amount for Meggie, no matter what she wanted. But he wouldn't dirty her with the truth about his dealings in Kane's Crossing.

A red curl danced across her chill-blushed cheek as she turned to him. "I imagine Deacon Chaney is having a good night."

The truth. Meggie was after it like a bee after a flower. Problem was, she didn't know how sour it would be.

"I imagine he is."

"Just think, all this time he had enough money tucked away to buy that big old department store. And here I thought he was living with his cranky son because he enjoyed it."

Oh, brother. "Playing the clueless snoop doesn't become you, Meggie."

"I'm curious. Especially if it concerns you."

He picked up a strawberry, moving it toward her mouth. Anything to stop these questions. "No worries, all right?"

She narrowed her green-as-cricket-wing eyes at him, ignoring the plump, red treat he offered. "You tell me that all the time. 'No worries.' Well, I am worried."

He ate the strawberry himself, buying a pause in the conversation. The last thing he wanted to do was to upset her. Maybe after he'd purchased the houses that rightfully belonged to the displaced families he'd tell her more. But, as of this moment, he wanted to keep Meggie out of his plans. It wouldn't be long until Kane's Crossing would welcome back those wrong-side-of-the-track citizens; Nick had spent most of the day in contact with his main office in Cincinnati, lighting a fire under his employees to close the deals on the individual lots.

Stubborn as ever, Meggie delicately picked a strawberry by its stem from the container, skimmed a curl from her lips and bit into the fruit, juice trickling from the side of her mouth.

Nick fought the urge to sip the wetness as it meandered to the crook of her chin, to nip and suck at her lips, slaking his thirst for her.

Meggie dabbed at her chin with a napkin, seeming totally unaware of his longing, thank God. He'd scare her to the other side of Kane's Crossing if she knew the power of his yearnings. He tried to distract himself by filling her plate with food.

As they ate, Meggie pointed to a cove of rocks banked into the hill to create a perfect hiding place. He recognized it immediately.

"Brings back a memory or two," she said, nibbling on a muffin. "Too bad they're not good memories."

His jaw clenched as he thought of Chad Spencer's shadow filtering over them as they hid from the King of Fools' posse. The pack had always razzed him for staying silent, for wearing raggedy clothes.

Things hadn't changed so much.

He still preferred a minimum of conversation and holes in his denim. And he'd still defend Meggie's honor, even if the stakes were much higher now.

Nick tried to relax, bending his legs so he could lean his arms on his thighs. "Let's think of other times. We didn't just spend that one day here."

"That's right." Meggie struggled to her knees, her eyes brightening.

It took everything Nick had to not reach out and help with her balance. He knew she'd want to take care of that on her own. Independent little cuss.

She continued. "Remember climbing Old Rufus over there?" She pointed to a massive oak, its thick trunk connecting to the hardy arms that'd held them, giving them an all-encompassing view of Kane's Crossing to the right.

"I remember swimming in the lake one night." He tried to hide a smile.

"I had my bathing suit on," she chided, lifting a brow at him. "But I recall that someone else didn't wear boxers. Or skivvies, for that matter."

Yep, things hadn't changed so much. "I got in some real trouble with the Renos when I trudged in at two in the morning."

"Bless Aunt Valentine's heart. She never said a word to me, even though I knew she'd been looking in her crystal ball all night, trying to see if I was okay."

''Think she really saw anything?''

Meggie raised her brows up and down, tilting her head to the side, taking Nick back a few years. He saw a barefoot girl dressed in wispy, sheer skirts, her long, coltish legs freckled and toasted by the sun. She'd worn scarves and flowers in her hair. She'd drawn temporary butterfly and peace sign tattoos on her skin with pink ink. She'd been free as a sunrise, bursting out in all directions with color and hope.

What he saw now twisted his heart even more. A woman dressed in baggy overalls and sweater shirt with a faded blue shawl draped around her shoulders, her skin a pale reminder of her days in the sun. Her eyes held the gleam of times past—a time when she'd swung from tree branches with carefree abandon, a time when she'd stood up to Chad Spencer, giving as good as she got.

She yawned, ruining the illusion.

He opened his arms to her, inviting her to share his warmth, his comfort.

Meggie leaned into him, conjuring memories of that fateful day when he'd been kicked out of Kane's Crossing.

One moment stood out more than all the rest, the endless minute when she'd peeked up at him through her red-tinged eyelashes, batting them until he thought she had something in her eyes. Then she'd asked that question.

Do you love me?

When he hadn't answered, he'd hurt her. Even now he remembered the sharp nip of discomfort with crystal clarity.

He looked down at her now, and she at him. The

recollection came rushing back; he could see it reflected in her eyes.

They were married. *Married,* for God's sake. What would he tell her if she asked again?

Do you love me?

Did he? He had no idea. He'd never encountered that kind of love in all his travels. Even the women he'd been with hadn't lent him insight into that mysterious emotion. What would love feel like? Would he know it when it happened?

He'd felt love for his foster family, but that had been different. It was what he felt for Meggie now. A willingness to die for them.

Was the other kind of love the same thing?

Dammit anyway. It was all a bunch of bull. He should concentrate on what he already knew. Justice. The need to even the odds and defend what was right.

Without the cold comfort of justice, he'd be lost.

Meggie's eyes turned from the color of summer grass to the green of his musty-smelling juvenile hall uniform. The night the sheriff had taken him away from the Renos, checked him into the Spencer County Center for Children and shoved him into a dank cell with a creaking cot and iron bars was the first night of the rest of his life.

After serving his time, Nick had gone on to foster home after home, some more of a nightmare than others. All places he knew he couldn't stay in.

As Meggie smiled at him, he glanced away, not wanting her to see his pain. He was doing his damnedest to erase it.

Her soft voice felt like a balm. "Maybe we shouldn't have come back here."

How could he say that being with her now, here, at

the scene of his last day in Kane's Crossing, was just what he needed? Being with Meggie seemed like a second chance, an opportunity to start his life over from the moment he decided to meet Spencer at Chaney's Drugstore to fight.

Words escaped him. Instead, he bent his head to touch his lips to hers, sealing his need for a second chance with the heat of his hunger.

He tasted strawberry juice on her chin, smelled a hint of cinnamon as he slid toward her ear to nibble and tongue her earlobe. She groaned beneath him, and he shifted her weight so she lay between his legs, her back against his chest.

He'd always held a soft place in his heart for Meggie, but now that part of him wanted to touch her, to feel her smooth, bare skin beneath the calluses on his palms. He took her shawl and spread it on the wind, guiding it to land over the front of her. He kissed the tender spot between neck and ear.

"Tell me to stop, Meggie."

She let out a jagged breath. "What for?"

She leaned into him as he traced his fingertips below the shawl, inside the gape of her overalls. He lifted her shirt, feeling the warmth of her skin, the crescent of her belly. He rubbed, the rasping of her body against his driving him on.

He buried his head in her strawberry-scented hair, making a blur of the sunset. After closing his eyes, he moved her shirt higher, cupping his hands over her soft breasts until she wiggled against him, making him pulse even more desperately against his jeans.

Meggie ran her hands up and over his shoulders, neck, into his hair, stretching, filling his palms. She'd certainly grown from girl to woman, and the dichotomy of being intimate on the grass of their childhood stomping grounds made him feel at once guilty and ready to make love right here, amid the landmarks of a more innocent time.

He pulled his mouth away from her, trying to control his longings. Meggie reached for him, bringing him back to her lips in a more heated kiss, their tongues moving in rhythmic time to her fingers strumming on his neck.

He broke away. "Meggie," he said, restraining his need to back her onto the ground and explore every inch of her body, "I'm not going to be able to help myself."

She laughed softly, her hand traveling down to the hole in the knee of his jeans. She slipped some fingers inside, dragging her nails over the back of his knee, almost making him explode with yearning.

She bit her lip, watching his reaction. "You're doing a pretty good job of helping yourself now."

Her touch trailed back up to his chest, swirling downward toward his belt line. He grasped her wrist before she could go farther. Gaze feverish, she glanced up at him. He let go of her as she backed away.

Beneath the shawl, he sensed movement, and he knew she was undoing the straps of her overalls. He heard the tinny clang of the buckles as they fell loose. She lifted up her shirt, maneuvered some more and— wonder of wonders—her industrial-strength bra peeked from the fringes of the blanket after she tossed it away.

Nick *couldn't* help himself. He gently pulled her back against him, smoothing his hands over her bare belly, her breasts. He fit a nipple between his fingers and rubbed, edging his other hand under the fullness of the opposite breast, pressing her back against his increasing hardness.

Meggie moaned beneath his touch, covering his hands with hers. They both moved down to her stomach, curving over it together, slipping under the roundness, testing what might lie beneath.

He caught his breath, thinking that he'd have given anything to have this baby be his own. But making love to the woman who was carrying this child wasn't going to magically change the father, even if that's how it'd been formed in the first place.

They didn't move for a moment. He wondered what was going through her mind. "Meggie, this isn't the place for what I want to do with you."

A tremble alerted him to her frustration. "Yeah, we've got quite a crowd watching," she said, the bite of sarcasm crushing the moment.

"Do you think I'd stop if I thought this was right?"

He immediately regretted his outburst. Dammit, that's why he shut the hell up most of the time.

Meggie pulled the shawl around her and sat up, depriving him of her body heat. He missed her scent, the pressure of her back against his chest, the feel of her soft skin. His arms missed her, too.

While she put herself together, he turned his back, trying to amend his words. "This just isn't the right place."

From behind him, he heard her voice floating on the November wind.

"Will it ever be?"

He wasn't so sure himself.

Chapter Eleven

Would there ever be a right time for her and Nick?

Meg couldn't answer that question. As she reclined in her old-fashioned, lion-pawed bathtub, she ran a sponge down her body, following the path Nick's hands had taken hours earlier.

The steady drip of the faucet tweaking into the strawberry-scented bathwater worked at her mind, pelting her conscience with thoughts she shouldn't have been thinking.

She'd acted without considering the consequences while they were picnicking at Cutter's Hill. She'd ignored every lesson she'd learned from Chad's ill treatment of her. Nick's sure touch could do that to a woman—make her lose her senses while stroking them.

Meg closed her eyes and relived the feel of his hands on her bare skin. She'd almost cried out with want of him, but knew it'd be best to hide her emotions. After all, Nick didn't love her.

Do you love him?

Oh, good. Now she was hearing voices in her head. Maybe this was another benefit of pregnancy, one that rivaled swollen ankles and those hemorrhoids she feared.

Well?

She couldn't answer herself. Love would mean giving her all, and she didn't know if Nick would accept that from her.

What a pair. Two people who hid secrets, even from the person who was supposed to support them throughout life.

Meg carefully got out of the tub, watched the water whisk down the drain, then toweled off. Afterward she dotted a herbal scent on her pulse points, smoothed her stubborn hair and slathered the same herbal-tinged lotion over her body. Before leaving the bathroom, she dressed in a baggy white nightgown that reminded her of Jane Eyre, all Gothic and lace.

Once in her room, she slid beneath the clean linen sheets of her bed, turning onto her left side. It was more comfortable in this position lately. No more snoozing on her belly or back. She'd miss the old ways.

Meg wiggled her tingling legs, unable to get comfortable.

Okay. Analyzing her sleeping positions wasn't working. She needed something else to distract her from Nick.

She stared out the window, thinking that the moon had holes in its surface.

Holes. Holes in jeans. Nick's jeans. Fantasy fulfilled

when she'd burrowed her hand inside and touched his
skin....

Now this was getting ridiculous. Wasn't there anything else to occupy her mind? Maybe she could debate
Nietzsche with herself, or maybe she could think about
the concept of eternity, how long it was...

An eternity without Nick. That's what this non-
slumber experiment was turning out to be.

Sigh. Then the hint of a creak. Another creak. Footsteps in the hall, coming to her door.

Stopping at her door.

Meg's heart started slamming; her head clouding,
her body buzzing. She wanted him so badly she ached
all over, as if from a fever.

The pause was interminable. Then another creak.

Oh, God. She couldn't let him get away. Not tonight.

"Nick?" Her voice sounded like a toad's, a croak
from the woods.

Silence. Had he heard her?

She tried again. "Is that you, Nick?"

Her door's crystal knob turned ever so slowly, the
hinges purring as Nick's body filled the door frame
with a dark silhouette. "Is everything okay, Meggie?"

No, most definitely not. She sat up in bed, her hair
tumbling over her eyes. She pushed her locks back over
her shoulder. "Sure, I'm fine. I..."

He wasn't moving, rooted like Old Rufus the oak
tree on Cutter's Hill. Meg wanted him to come closer.
She wanted to smell his leathery scent, feel his rough-
skinned hands on her back.

She tried to whisper. "Thank you for the cradle."

He walked into the room, shutting the door behind
him. Meg's stomach jumped.

"What?"

Success. She lowered her voice, so he'd have to come even closer. "The cradle. It's beautiful."

He stopped, inches from her bed, lingering at the side of it. His bulk cast a shadow over the outline of her shape, which was covered by a white, hand-embroidered comforter.

"What do you mean, Meggie?"

From what she could see of him in the dark, he appeared to be embarrassed. The only thing that would complete her suspicion is if he started shuffling his feet like an aw-shucks schoolboy.

"The cradle." She said it louder. "The cradle, you stubborn mule. The one that's just sitting in the workshop."

Thumbs in belt loops, his patented protective stance. Had she pushed him back?

"You're welcome. I'll move it to the nursery as soon as I can air it out."

His body language seemed to be shouting, "Is that all, ma'am?" Meg didn't know what to do. She wanted him in this bed with her, fulfilling the promise of their marriage. She wanted to say that she loved Nick without having the sentiment scare him silly, chasing him out of her life in the direction that so many had traveled before.

He watched her, not moving an inch. An encouraging sign. Her body began to throb under the pressure of his gaze.

"Make love with me, Nick," she whispered.

"Don't ask me to do that, Meggie."

She remembered the crush-iron grip of rejection in a little girl's heart—a little girl who'd asked her friend if he loved her while they'd hid among the rocks on the slant of Cutter's Hill.

She shrank back into the comfort of her pillow, pulling the covers up to her chin. "I understand. You aren't attracted to me in that way. I know, I'm grotesque with my stomach bulging out to Tombouctou and my face swollen like it's been stung by a swarm of bees—"

"Dammit, Meggie!" He bent to her, his hands cupping her face. "How can you say that? I want you more than anything in this world. But you have to understand—you're not mine to have."

"Of course I am." Why did she have the feeling that his crusade against Chad Spencer had something to do with his reluctance? "Does it have something to do with Chad?"

He stiffened and straightened.

His silence told her everything. "I'd do anything to change the father of my baby," said Meg, trying valiantly to control the tremor in her voice, yet hardly succeeding. "But that's just not possible. Why can't you forget about what he did, Nick?"

"Why can't you *remember?*" Barely restrained rage filled the space around him. "He ruined both our lives."

She pushed down the covers a little. "Oh, no. Not at all. Would you call this—" she motioned around the room, the house "—ruin? We can take disappointment and turn it into something wonderful. And it can start right here, right now."

He held on to her hand. "You really believe that."

"Yes, I do. And I believe that what happened on Cutter's Hill today wasn't just a case of insanity. I would've gladly become your wife in every sense if you'd just let me, Nick."

He hesitated. "But you're pregnant."

At one time Meg had thought making love while

baking a bun in the oven wasn't possible. But she'd done her research, and it'd be fine. She was also finding that her hormones were very open to the idea of intimacy with Nick. They had been ever since he'd hunkered into her bakery and scared away the customers with his glower.

"No worries, Nick Cassidy." She reached up.

Some kind of barrier broke within him. She could tell, because he leaned over her, fusing his lips to hers, maneuvering her body to one side so his weight wouldn't crush her.

She wove a leg through the juncture between his, running her hands down his back. She pulled his T-shirt from his pants, urging him to sit up and discard the flannel covering as well.

When he returned to her, he wore only his jeans, the feel of his bare chest against her body the stuff dreams were made of. Their music was the sounds of an old house: wind breathing under windowpanes and neglected cracks, thumps of an ancient tree as it knocked against the wall, the buzz of a still night outside. As his cheek wisped against her throat, her neck, she thought the most stirring sound of all was the rhythm of his breathing, gaining speed and intensity with every minute they touched.

She threaded her fingers through his hair, so soft, so carelessly wind-scuffed, and moaned low in her throat as he untied the ribbon at her collarbone, his mouth following the path of his fingertips.

She ran her nails up his spine, tracing the bumps while he kissed the pulse of her neck. "Did you ever think this old house would see such action?" she asked, laughing softly. She couldn't help it; she was happy enough to scream.

"I'm sure it has some stories to tell." He kissed her again, sending her heart racing to the stars.

Meg thought her protruding stomach might hamper their affection, but that wasn't so. Nick took care to keep his weight on his elbows, never leaning into her belly. He pulled back and reclined on his side, looking down at her, and slipped a hand under her gown, his touch skimming up the tender area at the back of her knee, the muscle-line of her thigh, her hip.

"You're so beautiful, Meggie," he whispered, his gravel-harsh voice scratching her soul with confidence. She'd thought he'd be turned off by her burgeoning body, but she was wrong. Thank goodness, she was wrong.

Slowly, he eased her bikini undies from her body, allowing his thumb to smooth into the damp space between her legs on the journey down. Meg hid her face in the pillow to cover a moan.

When the panties reached her ankles, she kicked them away. She rubbed a palm over his chest, over the hard bumps and valleys, then bent to kiss his nipple, biting softly.

He groaned, running his hands through her hair, fisting it gently, as she scratched his back, his stomach. She found the opening to his jeans, using her knuckles to trace the bulge straining against the material.

"Dammit, Meggie, you're going to drive me crazy."

"Likewise." She couldn't help the joy from sneaking into her voice. She'd never felt so wanted.

As she unbuttoned his pants, he explored her through the gown, dragging his fingertips over her arms, stomach, breasts. Especially her breasts. They were tender, but he seemed to understand, not pressing too hard.

He bent, fastening his lips to a breast, laving it with

his tongue, wetting her gown until she was sure that her pebbled nipples were outlined, even in the dark. His hands traveled her lower back, pressing her into him.

She wiggled against his firm body, making him drive his mouth against hers again in a kiss even more urgent. She took the opportunity to ease her fingers inside his jeans, feeling the length of him as she shucked off the material. They thumped onto the floor, the sound echoing through the room.

She could feel him through the thin gown, feel him pressing against her thigh, testing the area between her legs.

A moment of panic seized her. What if he left her after tonight? What if this man broke her heart again?

She used her hands to push away from Nick. Her bed's canopy netting hovered above her like an attacking mist.

Nick cupped her jawline, his breathing raspy, cutting through the night. "What's wrong?"

What exactly was wrong? Wasn't she the one who'd called him into her room? Her body still cried out for him, so why was she hesitating?

She reached down, pulling her gown over her body, tossing it to the side. "Nothing's wrong."

Nothing was ever wrong with them.

With a strong oath, he palmed a breast, softly kneading, bending his head to take her into his mouth, making her melt into his body. She moved against him, holding his head as he kissed and swirled his tongue against her. Then he traveled lower, running a tongue into her belly button, tracing it down the line on her belly, lower...lower.

She caught her breath, squeezing her eyes shut, hand reaching over her head to grasp at the brass headboard.

He caressed her stomach, tracing fingertips down the sides, over the top.

Then he was back, gaze to gaze. He used a finger to enter her, preparing her for what was to come.

"You're ready," he said, kissing her again.

They fit together perfectly, their skin sleek, rubbing against each other with ever-increasing friction. When he entered her, Meg gasped. He filled her so completely.

They moved together, her legs wrapped around his, his weight balanced on his arms so he could join his lips to hers.

A storm was building within her, so fierce that she thought she'd burst. Thunder pounded through her body, rattling limbs. Lightning flew across her vision, blinding her with singular intensity. Both elements combined, throwing her out of body to scream across pale blue skies the color of Nick's eyes.

And then they lay in each other's arms, bodies entwined, breathing evenly matched. She traced his firm jawline as he smoothed a strand of hair from her forehead.

Then there was silence and, for once, she didn't mind.

After another hour of cuddling, kissing and napping, Nick's low voice broke the silence.

"We weren't protected."

She shifted, pulling the covers up over her chest, feeling the weight of his hand on what she used to call a waist. Through the fog of sleep, she couldn't quite assimilate what he was saying. "What do you mean?"

''No condom.'' He lowered his tone. ''But I've always worn one before. And I've been tested. It should be okay.''

A spark of worry lit through her. Yet, if she couldn't trust Nick, who could she trust? ''Well, it's not like I'll get pregnant.''

Her attempt at humor fell flat. She added, ''I'll go to the doctor tomorrow, just to make us both feel better.''

Maybe he was afraid that Chad had given her some disease. Heck, how could she blame him, even if she'd gotten a clean bill of health from her own doctor?

''If it helps, sure,'' he said.

They didn't talk after that. Meg wondered if he'd lain awake, beating himself up over the lack of protection.

His breathing evened out, and, after a while, hers did, as well.

At the first sign of dawn Meg came awake, pleasantly surprised to see that Nick was still huddled next to her. As faint light streamed through the window, she quietly turned her body toward Nick—her husband.

This was the perfect opportunity to study him. Really study him, because she'd never had the chance before.

Wicked woman, she thought to herself, tugging down the white sheet so she could peruse his body.

With the soft sunrise suffusing his form, he looked chiseled out of stone, hard as the dawn-coated mountains of San Diego County. But she knew he was softer than that. She'd learned that lesson well last night.

She grinned, her body responding to the memories even now. She pulled the sheet a bit lower, exposing his back, the marbled smoothness of his muscles as they tapered into a lean waist. Farther down—

Wait.

Farther down there was something she needed a closer look at.

Tiny puckered marks resembling old blisters. The shape and texture reminded her of the circular glow of someone sucking a cigarette down to ash.

As she traced her finger over one, she found others, all over his waistline and lower back.

Good Lord, what were these?

She touched one again, harder this time. Nick awakened with a start, turning around, backhand, to seize her wrist, his blue eyes wild as a hot, stray spark.

"What are you doing, Meggie?"

His tone brooked no gentleness.

"Cigarette marks. These are cigarette marks." She couldn't stop her words from knocking together, trembling like leaves in a storm.

He hurled a curse across the room, tightening the sheet around his lower body. "It's nothing. Nothing."

"It sure is something. Dammit, Nick Cassidy, how did you get these?"

He sat up, knees crooked until it made the sheet a tent. With undue force, he ran his hands over his face, five-o'clock shadow whiskers grating against the harsh touch.

Meg got out of bed, grabbed her gown and tugged it over her body. Crossing her arms over her chest, she perched on the side of the mattress, somewhat afraid of this man and the thunderous murder of his gaze. "This time you can't push aside my questions. You can't play it off like it's no big deal. The proof's right there, Nick. I'm not going to let up on this one."

"Dammit, Meggie."

''Tell me.'' Nausea nudged at her throat. Did she really want to hear this?

He shook his head, staring out the window. ''They're burns from one of my foster homes. The kids who lived there used to hold me down and burn me.''

Meg couldn't believe such a thing had happened to Nick. ''Did your foster parents do anything?''

''They didn't know.''

She couldn't say anything but, ''Why did those kids do this to you?''

''Who the hell knows why?'' A bitter laugh. ''Because I was defiant, because I got good grades in school. Because I was me.''

Because I was me. How many times had she thought the same thing over the years? She'd always blamed what happened in San Diego on herself, always accepted the punishments with resignation. It was her fault. It always would be.

Nick was watching her, faint red circles under his eyes to match the burn marks. He said, ''The wages of sin never stop, do they?''

She gasped, wondering if he could read her mind.

''But I don't remember ever sinning this badly,'' he said softly, voice a low rasp of pain.

She crawled to him, enveloping him in her arms, his head to her breast. What could she do to make him feel better?

Share your pain.

That voice again. Wouldn't it go away? She wasn't about to share her secret. It was too awful. Chad would use it against her, Nick would hate her.

They'd been physically intimate last night. But she couldn't bring herself to be emotionally joined. Never.

Say something, anything to get it out of your mind.

"Why would they put you in a home like that?"

She felt his lips moving against her as he talked, his voice muffled by the contact. "It was right after juvenile hall, after I reportedly blew up the drugstore." His voice shook. "My new parents thought I needed strict discipline. Thought I needed to remember what I'd done. One really big, older boy thought it'd be funny to fight fire with fire. He and a couple other foster kids thought they'd take matters into their own hands, without my guardians' knowledge. I suppose the marks were supposed to remind me of the explosion."

"Oh, God." She wished she could do something for him. But there was nothing. Nothing at all. "How long did you have to stay?"

"Too long. My social worker got me out as soon as she knew what was happening, but I never did find a real home."

And it was all Chad Spencer's fault for framing a poor foster kid. She could hear the accusation in every syllable. Somehow, she understood his rage.

He continued. "Spencer took away the only home I ever had, the only parents who wanted to accept me, adopt me. Do you know what it feels like to have that snatched from you?" He shook his head, gritting his jaw. "Every time a cigarette hissed into my skin, I'd think of Spencer. Every time I'd count my burns, I'd count the days until I saw him again."

"What are you saying?"

He pulled away, evidently not caring that the sheet had gaped to reveal more burns on his hips. His gaze held all the fire of his scars. "I'm saying that Chad Spencer is going to suffer."

As he got out of bed and walked through the door, Meg bowed her head, tasting tears of anguish as they rolled down her face.

Chapter Twelve

Through the course of several days, Nick berated himself for telling Meggie about his awful secret. He shrank back from the soft, pitying sheen of her tearful eyes. She'd even closed the bakery to stay home with him, to make him happy about something in life, he supposed.

As he and Meggie sat in the attic, going through trunks for more of Valentine's old clothes that Meggie could wear during her last trimester, Nick avoided her gaze and tried to keep the conversation aimed toward less angst-ridden subjects.

A light rain pattered on the pane-glass window while Meggie held up a flowery dress, her belly pooching the material. She laughed and grabbed a straw hat from a seamstress's dummy, its blank face showing no bitterness at the loss of accessories. Meggie twirled around, modeling her new ensemble.

Nick's body reacted to this innocent gesture, remembering their night together. He hadn't made a move toward her since then, and he would catch a question in her sheepish smile whenever night approached.

Meggie grinned, standing in front of Nick, who was seated on the wooden-plank floor. "Am I the picture of a Sunday walk in the park or what?"

The only thing he could imagine was slipping every inch of clothing from her body. He nodded in response, running a hand over his mouth to hide any lurking hint of surrender.

"Well," said Meggie, tossing the hat and dress into a growing pile of clothes, "thank goodness Aunt Valentine was a big-boned woman. These should last me through the pregnancy."

He wanted to steer around the small talk, ease her onto a mattress, spread her red hair into a sunset fan and make love with her again. Trouble was, he wouldn't let himself, not when he'd only revert to form and leave the relationship before she lost interest in him. It'd happened before with every other woman he'd dated; it'd happened with his foster families. Nick Cassidy had been born without staying power and, somehow, he always made sure he controlled the hurt before it got to *him* first.

Making love was one thing; keeping it around was definitely another. He didn't know if he could manage the second part.

He stood, brushing the dust from his jeans. "I'll get to work on the nursery."

"Work, work, work. You, my man, need to have a little fun." She came over and held his hands, swinging them back and forth.

There it was again, the expression that asked, "Why

haven't you touched me since *that* night?'' How could he give a straight answer without hurting her?

He said, ''The devil's best apprentice is a pair of idle hands. Or something like that.'' He'd heard the phrase somewhere before, and he had a bad feeling it'd been shouted in his ear since time began.

Meggie tilted her head. ''Whoever told you that must've never stopped to smell the roses.'' She stood on tiptoe, planting a soft kiss below his jawline.

Nick's stomach twisted, and he watched the sway of her hips as she sauntered to a massive, teakwood chest, gargoyles carved into the top.

She ''Oofed'' while lifting the lid. Nick stepped forward, intending to help her.

''I can manage,'' she said.

''Naturally.''

As she riffled through the chest's contents, exotically colored silk scarves, violet-hued crystal perfume jars and golden costume jewelry began to litter the floor. ''I used to play in this attic all the time. I stopped after I came back from San Diego, though.''

Nick rested an arm on an old mahogany player piano, its yellowed keys sprinkled with dust. ''Why did you stop?''

Her faraway gaze fixed on a web-rained corner of the room. ''Maybe I just outgrew the need to dress like a Gypsy girl. It started feeling foolish, making me feel like even more of an outcast, I guess.''

She'd always looked like a flower among weeds, but Nick didn't dare say so. ''I miss those days.''

Her shoulders stiffened. ''You were right about not being able to get them back.''

True, but you could make sure people paid for past mistakes, just like Spencer would pay for his.

A dusky orange veil landed in his lap. When he looked up, he caught Meggie in the act of flinging a blue one in his face. "What did I do to deserve this onslaught?" he asked.

"I talked to Rachel on the phone, and she heard the most interesting rumor."

He tossed the material back at her. "What now? Hasn't Kane's Crossing wagged their tongues enough this year?"

"Evidently not. Deacon Chaney's got a big mouth, Nick. You knew that before you gave him the department store."

She was guessing, but he knew he shouldn't have trusted the old man to keep a secret. All he'd been trying to do was make up for the damage of the drugstore incident, even if he hadn't been the one to blow it up.

"Chaney's delusional," said Nick, hoping his clenched hands didn't betray the truth.

Meggie played with a scarf, tying a teal one in her hair, the curls dancing over the foamy material. "Deacon, my pal, also said you'd started construction on that arcade by Cutter's Lake."

He held up a finger to object, but Meggie's voice beat him to the punch.

"*And* you bought the Renos' old home, intending to turn it into an orphanage." A strange pride blushed her face.

"Any other ridiculous gossip you want to run by me?" His employees in the main office were going to get a dressing down for giving Chaney too much information. He'd told them to mete out only enough data to make running the department store easy. Besides, he'd only recently decided to convert his old home into a shelter for abused children. It was the right thing to do.

When Meggie flashed him a goofy, I'm-so-dang-happy-with-you grin, he continued, "That house needs to be utilized for something."

She used the trunk to help her stand and came over to slide her arms around him, her face pressing against his chest, her belly rubbing against an area that needed no encouragement. "You're quite a man, Nick Cassidy. I just wish you'd tell me these things yourself. Having to find it out through the grapevine is a hard pill for a wife to swallow."

Wife. Yes, she was his wife in every way. Almost. "I'm working on it, Meggie. But what you hear, you might not like."

"I'm willing to accept everything about you." She looked up at him, green eyes filled with something that surpassed friendliness. "Even the stories behind the scars."

More stories than he cared to admit to. What exactly was he afraid of? That Meggie would leave him? He'd tried to set up their marriage so that emotions wouldn't matter. But the thought of her rejecting him was unthinkable, as horrific as finding out that the only foster family who'd ever loved him was gone.

The old Nick came creeping back into his mind, suggesting, whispering, *Drive her off before she can do it to you. Take control. Don't allow anyone to hurt you again.*

Meggie's voice overshadowed his conscience. "You're so good deep inside, Nick, even under that hard shell. For one thing, look at what you're doing for the community. People are talking all over town, coming to think of you the way I do. And I'm so proud of you for staying out of fights. You've learned to control your temper, and I know that's hard."

She was giving him too much credit. He'd merely restrained his anger in front of her by not talking about it.

She added, "Deacon Chaney is telling everyone who comes into his store about Chad detonating the bomb. He's clearing your name."

That much was true. Over the past week or so, citizens had been smiling at him, greeting him with such American-pie sentiments as, "A good morning to you, Mr. Cassidy" or "Welcome back to Kane's Crossing, Mr. Cassidy." He should've known Deacon was talking him up. He should've never trusted a man who used to dress like a bug-eyed scarecrow.

Nick felt a bitter sense of victory. When it came right down to it, he didn't care too much about the town's opinion. Months ago he thought it would matter more.

Then again, he didn't know if anything would cause him to feel good about himself. At night, when the wind and house were quiet, he could still hear the whispers of the past.

Be seen and not heard, boy...

Shut up, you stupid little idiot. Anything you have to say ain't worth the breath it comes out on.

He pressed his lips to Meggie's forehead, breathing in her scent. She'd been baking apple bread in their kitchen today, and the aromas of cinnamon and fruit tempted him.

He tightened his hold on her, feeling her body respond to his. She pulled against him, running her nails down his back. They swayed together, lost in the moment.

Out of the blue, a coatrack swooped toward them.

Nick lunged forward and caught it before it slammed Meggie in the head.

"What the—" He untangled a scarf that was draped over Meggie's shoulder from one of the rack's gnarled fingers. He held it up for her inspection.

She put a hand over her heart. "And here I thought it was a chaperone, like at a school dance." She laughed. "I'm such an idiot sometimes."

Meggie watched as Nick's face darkened, as if storm clouds were gathering in his eyes. She stepped back, balling a scarf in front of her stomach.

He shoved the coatrack back to its place. "*Idiot*'s a pretty strong word."

"I'm sorry, I didn't mean…"

He held up a hand, halting her explanation. "It's okay."

Where had the other Nick gone? In an instant, the man with the gunslinger stance and barricaded gaze had returned. Taking a deep breath, she rushed to him, embracing him as if he was disappearing into thin air. "Please tell me what's wrong. I want to know… everything."

"I told you before. You don't want to hear."

But she did. And from the way he was holding her, he just might be willing to share a little of himself.

He let out a shuddering sigh. "All right, then. They used to call me 'idiot' when I was a kid. Remember how I told you when we were young that my real parents dropped me off on the hospital steps when I was a baby?"

"Yes." It'd sounded like a warped fairy tale, but she'd believed anything he told her.

"It was all a crock." He hugged her fiercely. "After I could afford to spend money however I wanted, I set

out to find my real parents. I guess I thought they
would accept me back after all these years. So one day,
after I found out where they lived, I crept up the stairs
to this creaky shack off a deserted highway. I should've
known then that I was in for it.''

Meggie looked into his troubled eyes, smoothing
back the hair from his face as he continued.

''A woman answered the door. I had no idea who
she was, but she seemed hundreds of years old. Then
she smiled, and I realized it was my mom. That smile
was the only glimmering moment I remembered from
the past. Then a man started to yell in the background,
over the noise of TV wrestling.''

She could hear the bullet-bang of his heart through
his shirt. Meg held him tighter, rubbing his back.

''I recognized that voice immediately, except this
time it wasn't screaming 'idiot' or 'waste of life' at
me. When I saw this old man, leaning back on a battered couch, I knew it was my dad. And, you know
what? The man took great pride in telling me that he
thought I was dead or in jail. At that second, I saw my
life through a little boy's eyes, hiding under the table
while he berated me during a thunderstorm, or locked
me in a closet for days just because I'd looked at him
the wrong way. There was nothing to say. I left.''

How awful to have your own parents reject you.
Meg knew that story well, but she'd be damned if she
would share it. She respected Nick for his courage,
more than she thought possible, especially since he felt
he could lay his burdens on her. Her heart swelled with
the absolute certainty of love.

He absently played with her hair. ''My old social
worker filled me in on the rest—how she took me out
of the house when I was five, how one of my foster

families had tried to make me feel better by telling me the hospital story. It all fell into place, and I knew I had to do something to correct the past, especially after the car accident.''

Meg squeezed his firm waistline. ''You've got more bravery than I could imagine.'' And she hated herself for it, because she had none.

''Not by a long shot, Meggie. You're the most courageous person I know.'' He leaned back, using his thumb to trace her lips.

She shut her eyes, trying to hold back trembles of desire. It'd been too long since they'd made love, and she was crazy with the need for him.

She whispered, ''Why can't you care as much about me as you do about what Kane's Crossing thinks?''

Immediately she regretted the words. They'd rushed out without proper thought. Her guts fisted at what he might say to her.

Instead of words he took her hand and led her down the stairs.

To his bedroom.

And when they got there, they made love until her body sang, until every pore of her skin exploded with sky-scraping bursts of light and sound.

Then, as he fell asleep with his hand draped over her stomach, his warm breath buzzing the back of her neck, Meg saw it.

The baby picture, propped up on his nightstand, the child's eyes sparkling with the fireworks display of an infant's happiness, his toothless smile all gums and giggles.

Evidently, Nick wondered about her secrets, as well.

Meg squeezed shut her eyes, trying to block out the

photo with a wall of tears, knowing that having to tell Nick about her past was the price of love.

A week later Nick glanced at himself once again in the passenger side mirror of his truck, groaning at the split lip, the half-shut eye that was even now swelling into a fleshy pool of grape jelly.

Hell, at least Junior and Sonny looked worse than he did.

His truck engine sputtered to a stop, gliding into its parking spot in the garage.

Deacon Chaney, dressed in a three-piece suit and tie, his gray hair slicked back with a spicy oil, rested his arm on the steering wheel. "Can't believe it, but this baby drives like a dream."

Nick leaned his head against the window, procrastinating. When Meggie found out that he'd gotten into a fight, she'd flip. She'd never allow him the pleasure of sliding his hands over her sweet body again.

Man, he was in deep trouble.

Deacon got out of the truck and helped Nick up the stairs and through the kitchen screened door. Something good was cooking, smelling of stewed beef, carrots, celery, potatoes and green beans. Meggie had all but shut down the bakery, thank goodness, but she hadn't lost the flair for creating culinary magic.

"Stew," said Deacon, depositing Nick into a chair and rubbing a circle on his beanbag stomach. "Daggone, I miss Meg's bakery. Not that I'd have time to visit much more anyway with you being such a taskmaster."

Deacon grabbed a napkin and handed it to Nick, who used it to prod his lip. Still bleeding.

"If you don't like running the Mercantile, just tell me," said Nick, his words slightly muffled.

"Oh, no, I like it just fine." Deacon smiled smugly. "I like even more that you're admitting to buying the Spencers' property."

"I haven't admitted squat."

The scent of magnolias filled the room, overwhelming dinner's aroma. Meggie's voice followed.

"You're home!"

She gracefully stepped onto the kitchen tile, sheer violet, indigo and green material decorating her body. She looked like an Arabian-nights dream with the sheer swaths dripping over her stomach, barely concealing the glow of her skin. Costume jewelry Gypsy coins shimmered in her red hair, sounding like chimes on the wind. She leaned against the wall, a saucy grin on her face.

Then she saw Deacon. "Oh, Lord!" And ducked into the next room.

For his part, Deacon had the grace to blush and turn around, tugging nervously on his tie. "Moves pretty fast for a pregnant gal."

Nick held back a laugh, but sobered quite rapidly when the sting of his lip kicked in. "Deacon, if you say a word of this to anyone..."

"Oh, no. Not me."

Meggie peeked into the kitchen, coins shimmying in her curls. When she saw Deacon wasn't looking, she eased farther into the room, still covering herself with the wall. Then she got a load of Nick's wounds.

"Oh, no, Nick. What happened?"

He expected that tone of voice, that disappointed now-you've-done-it drone. His first instinct was to say, "Nothing," but they were beyond that now. Ever since he'd told her about the cigarette burns and his real parents, he couldn't find it within himself to go back to keeping secrets.

All except one.

Deacon stepped up for him. "Meg, it wasn't his fault. After I closed up, Sonny and Junior took it into their heads to jump me outside the Mercantile. Well, lucky for me that Nick was at the store, checking up on things today. Before Sonny could clamp his mouth shut, Nick told them to scoot. I can't fight worth beans, but you should've seen your husband—"

Nick shot him a silencing look.

Deacon shrugged, a grateful expression on his face. "I always knew he wasn't the one who blew up my store. That cretin Chad Spencer started bragging about framing Nick the day after it happened. But Sheriff Carson could've cared less. Everyone could've cared less." He smiled. "You came back to right things, though. I wasn't sure at first, but you're doing it, boy."

Nick peered through his good eye at Meggie, who was gazing at him so warmly that it captured his breath in his chest.

He couldn't believe it, but he almost felt decent about himself. A faint seed of pride had been planted when Meggie had agreed to marry him, to accept his help, and it'd been growing ever since, watered and fed by her touch and smiles.

"Deacon," she said, "may I be alone with my husband?"

A spark lit in Nick's chest, firing his heart.

"I should think so," said the elderly man. He began to walk out. "And one more thing. The Jones family stopped into the store today. They're moving back to Kane's Crossing. Seems as if someone—" he stopped and cleared his throat "—bought their house back from Chad Spencer and gave it to them. Now, I know the Spencers are scrambling with their fancy lawyers to get their properties back, but what a hell of a gesture."

Deacon nodded his head, glanced meaningfully at Nick, then left.

Nick hung his head, hearing Meggie's hair accessories clank against each other as she walked into the room.

"I'm glad to hear the Jones family is returning." She paused. "You?"

"Don't know them."

"Yeah." She tilted his face upward, concern in her eyes as she inspected his wounds. Without comment, she gathered ice, separated it into two bags and covered their chill with small towels.

As he held the coldness to his wounds, she left, returning shortly with medicines to clean his scrapes.

She removed the ice pack from his eye and set to work on dabbing antibacterial ointment on the wound. He sucked in his breath when she touched a particularly tender spot. His hands shot up to clench the material by her hips. Scarves wisped away to reveal more skin, and he couldn't help the resulting arousal.

The stew pot lid started banging against the pot, clanking, wanting attention. It went unanswered.

Nick couldn't stand the silence. "I was only helping out Deacon. Those maggots wanted to fight an old man."

"I know," Meggie said softly. She replaced the ice and went to work on his lip.

When she'd finished, he held on to her hips, resting his head against her stomach, feeling as if she'd healed more than just physical wounds. "I'm not busted?"

Her fingers played with his hair, making him sleepy, content. "How could I be angry about that? And you're not adding one very important thing. Gary Joanson wasn't there."

"Yeah?"

"Yeah. I think you converted at least one Chad Spencer disciple to your side."

He wasn't so sure of that. He'd seen Gary lingering in the background, not participating, yet not stopping his friends, either.

Nick trailed his hands under her veiled material, fingertips against the supple skin of her waist. He heard her catch her breath, ease closer to him until he could press his cheek against her belly again.

Meggie said, "You're incredible."

Sure. If that was true, then why couldn't he bring himself to tell her everything? That he wasn't just being a martyr and buying Kane's Crossing property out of the goodness of his heart? That he'd actually entertained thoughts of revealing the baby's paternity to Chad, just to cause trouble between him and his new fiancée?

"I bought those houses," he said, before thinking enough to stop himself. "And I'm buying more."

And it's not merely because I'm a good guy.

She'd be horrified if she knew how black it got in his heart, if she could step into the pit of his soul to fight the demons that lurked there.

As she smiled down at him, he felt like backing away. It was in her eyes—a certain reservation about his violent nature mixed with the willingness to travel within him, so she could witness every ugly mess he'd ever left. He didn't want her to see everything. What she already knew was enough.

She pulled him to his feet, shutting off the stove and leading him toward his bedroom. His pulse crashed in his ears, wave upon wave of urgency pulling him under.

The bed loomed, inviting and all-encompassing. He was losing himself to her.

When she sat him on the mattress, he waited for her to follow. But she remained standing and reached for the baby picture he kept waiting on his nightstand.

Chapter Thirteen

Meg knew it was time to tell him her most vile memory. He'd trusted her enough with his stories, and, if she truly loved him, she'd do the same.

She grabbed the baby picture, staring at it while finding the right words. She looked at Nick, finding him watching her with an understanding slant to his cut lip, a sympathetic glow in the one eye that wasn't swelling shut.

He put the ice bag against the bruise before she could remind him. They'd come to know each other well—especially on the physical level—but she was about to take it a step farther.

"I'm not sure if I can get this all out without breaking down." She sat on the bed, next to her husband.

He rested a reassuring hand on her opposite shoulder, fingering a strand of her hair. Suddenly, dressed in this playful harem-girl get-up, she felt vulnerable.

But telling Nick about her secret would be a form of healing, much like the ointment and ice he was using to soothe his wounds.

She exhaled, feeling a slight quaking that began in her stomach and spread to her limbs. "I'm scared to death that if this gets out, Chad will take the baby from me."

"It can't be that bad."

He'd change his tune in a minute. "It's so horrible that I've tried to believe another girl did it. But then I remember the feeling of holding…"

She placed the picture in his lap, as if trying to distance herself once again.

Nick skimmed his finger under her chin to direct her gaze to his. His eyes were a pale calm, the blue of a quiet summer sky. "Just tell me."

The shaking continued, intensifying. She crossed her arms over her chest, trying to still the terror.

Harsh images crossed her mind, flashing over her sight like distant stars falling to their deaths. Could she tell him what had happened after he'd been escorted out of Kane's Crossing?

He flashed her a bruised grin, and Meg knew she'd do anything for this man.

She exhaled, then began in a whisper. "When I came back home that summer, my mom had delivered her baby. They named him Jacob. And he was the most adorable child, Nick, always laughing and gurgling." She paused, smiling with the memory. "Even if he got a lot of the attention I used to have, how could I not love him with all my heart? I remember sneaking into his room to watch him coo and kick his little feet in the air. I gave him baths and fed him that mushy baby food with the plastic-coated spoons."

"Like the ones we bought," added Nick, probably thinking he was helping her.

Agony tore her heart into pieces. Meg didn't want to associate Jacob and the baby she now carried.

She almost lost her courage, but Nick slid her hand into his, giving it a reassuring squeeze.

"I can do this," Meg said, avoiding his gaze.

Another squeeze. "You can do anything," he said.

She loved him for saying that, but darkness shadowed her once more as she continued. Her voice wavered. "I guess we all have our share of those teenage moments. You know, with our parents. Everything's a drama at that age. I'd accuse my mom and dad of loving Jacob more than they loved me. But never for a minute did I want anything to happen to my little brother."

She looked longingly at Jacob's picture, hardly minding that her voice was pleading with her husband, pleading for him to understand. "I never wanted anything to happen."

Nick's other arm tightened around her. "Meggie, I know you'd never do anything to intentionally harm someone."

Her throat burned, but the tears didn't come. Not yet. The threat of tears had haunted her for years, but crying would only bring back the blaring hurt she'd stifled. The pain that was creeping up on her even at this moment.

The only things holding her together were Nick's comforting arm, the pressure of his hand holding hers.

"We haven't gotten to the worst part yet." She grabbed the picture, put it facedown on the bed. "One night I was assigned big-sister baby-sitting duty. It was the worst night of my life."

Jacob's sparkling blue eyes flew through her thoughts, bringing back the terror of that evening.

"My parents trusted me to keep Jacob safe. They'd even left two other kids with me that night since my mom and dad had gone out to dinner with another couple. I had to take care of Jacob and two little boys, running around the house in their cowboy hats, yelling, throwing baby toys against the walls. A baby-sitter's nightmare.

"So, thank goodness, at one merciful point, the two other children fell asleep in front of the television. One of them had smeared food on Jacob while they were eating and I didn't want my parents to see that the situation wasn't under control, perfect. Just like my grades at school. 'Everything in shipshape,' as my dad would say. After all, I was fourteen, an adult. It was expected."

Nick's soft, low voice broke in. "Sounds like they expected a lot out of you."

The first tear rushed out of her eye, hard as crystal, encasing years of despair. "This is tearing me apart to tell you, Nick."

"Hey," he said, enveloping her in a hug. "You don't have to."

They sat on the bed for a moment, the reprieve hardly assuaging Meg's guilt. She had to tell someone. And Nick was the one who deserved to know.

Her voice was muffled by his shirt, but, to Meg, the words echoed everywhere. "The water in the bathtub was the perfect temperature. Not too deep, not too hot. Jacob was smiling at me, waving his hands and feet, and splashing at the water. This is so strange, but I can almost smell the baby bath gel."

She stopped as the memory of that night came full force, sneaking up on her back, knifing her with guilt.

"One of the other children came up behind me, in the doorway.... Have you ever seen those *Friday the Thirteenth* movies, with Jason in the hockey mask?"

"Yeah."

"Well, that little kid, he started yelling, 'I'm Jason Voorhees, and I'm going to kill everyone!' And I whipped my head around to tell him to calm down, to go back to sleep. To do something. But he was holding what looked like a knife."

"Hell," Nick said, pulling her even closer. It was as if he could predict what was coming next.

By now, the words were rushing out of Meg's mouth, as unstoppable as the tears scorching her cheeks, marking her with shame. "I couldn't see anything I was so afraid, but I remember him running away from me, toward his brother in the family room. I remember his brother screaming, like he was being stabbed.

"I wasn't thinking straight. I mean, really, looking back, it hadn't seemed like the water would've been deep enough to drown Jacob."

She choked, unable to go on.

Nick cursed under his breath. As she shook with sobs and memories that had been bottled for much too long, she thought she felt the heat of his tears wetting her hair.

She tried to talk again, to explain more, but he placed a finger over her lips.

"You don't have to go on, Meggie."

"Don't you see?" she said, words scraping her throat raw. "I wasn't in time. After I chased that boy down, after I took that silver baby comb away from him, I came to my senses and ran to the bathroom. I thought I'd never get there, but, when I did..."

A long, wrenching sob escaped her soul, lasting the space of all the years she'd hated herself for killing her brother.

Nick held her, and she latched onto his arms as if they would save her.

Eons seemed to pass and, with her eyes burning, she looked up, trying to avoid Nick.

He tipped a finger under her chin, leading her to his compassionate gaze. The breath left her body when she saw the red haze lingering in his eyes, as blistering as the scars on his body.

"Forgive yourself, Meggie."

She sobbed once more, unable to control her emotions. "I can't.

"Please, Meggie." His voice shook, jarring her, too.

She backed away from him, hiding her face in her hands. "You didn't see his little body, floating facedown in the water. You didn't hear my parents saying that I'd always been jealous of him, I'd never wanted Jacob around. That it was my fault."

"Listen, Meggie." Rage warped his voice. "Your parents shouldn't have left a fourteen-year-old home alone with an infant and two hellion boys. Hell, I know how kids can be. If the blame's to be placed anywhere, it should be on your parents. And they probably know it."

"You don't understand," she said. "I *can't* forgive myself."

Nick smoothed his lips against her forehead. "It's in the past. It's all right. It'll be all right."

She shuddered. "I don't know."

"Try to think of something good, Meggie. You came

to live with Aunt Valentine after that, and *she* forgave you. Didn't she?''

A lump stuck in her throat. "Yes, she did. She'd hug me, and say, 'We all make mistakes, but the miracle is in forgiveness,' and I remember thinking that her magnolia perfume almost obliterated what I'd done. But it never lasted. The memory of Jacob's lifeless face always came back.''

"I forgive you, if that means anything.''

He'd said it so sheepishly, obviously not realizing that it meant the world. And that was a start.

She took his face in her hands, loving the bruises, loving the scars and wounded gaze. God, she wanted to tell him that she loved him, to give him everything inside her.

No, Nick didn't love her. He was acting as a friend should, supporting her, feeling sorry for her.

Softly she said, "You don't think this story makes my having this baby a bad choice? If Chad knew about this, he'd—''

"Why would he know?''

Relief flooded through her. "You won't say anything?''

Nick simply took her in his arms again, silent as a secret.

Meg sank into him, thinking that maybe forgiving herself wouldn't be so impossible after all. Not as long as Nick believed in her.

A few moments passed. Nick wanted to say something to comfort her, to cleanse her of the awful accusations she probably had littering her conscience. "I think you'll do a great job of taking care of this child. You'll be the perfect mother.''

She choked on a sob, and he thumbed away a tear. "Meggie, let it go."

Let it go.

Why was he preaching something he couldn't do himself?

She said, "When I first found out I was pregnant, I was petrified. I wondered how I would be able to take care of someone as small and frail as Jacob when I'd failed before. Then, I was sitting in the parlor, and that magnolia perfume..." She blushed. "You know what I mean. It was almost like Aunt Valentine was here, convincing me that I needed to forget the past. At that point, I realized that maybe...by succeeding with this child, I could make up for Jacob's death."

Her gaze burned with conviction. "That's why no one is ever going to take away my child. I'm going to give him or her everything I don't have from my parents."

"No one's going to take the baby. Not if I can help it." And he actually believed what he was saying.

The tick-tocking of the hallway grandfather clock marked their silence. He held her closer.

Would his revenge plan for Chad Spencer leave Meggie childless? Nick's hatred of the man was so intense that he didn't know if he could control himself when they finally came face-to-face. What if he couldn't keep her secrets to himself? What if, in one forgetful, revenge-driven moment, ruining Spencer's life became the most important thing to him?

With a start, Nick realized that Meggie and the baby could've surpassed Spencer. He'd come to Kane's Crossing for one reason—to bring the golden boy down. To show him how much it hurt to lose what you loved most in life.

But, now, his priorities had taken a U-turn. Protecting Meggie had always been important, but lately…

No. He couldn't lose sight of justice. If he didn't make Spencer pay, who would? He'd convinced himself that he was some vengeful guardian of this mission, that he was the only one who'd bring about karma. It was unthinkable that Spencer would go unpunished. He wouldn't be able to live, knowing that the man had gotten off scot-free for his crimes.

When he looked down at Meggie again, he saw the only thing that could obliterate his plans for Chad Spencer. She gazed at him as if he was the greatest man in the world. He couldn't stand it, because it wasn't true.

It was the same expression she'd had on her face that afternoon on Cutter's Hill when she was twelve.

"I love you, Nick Cassidy," she whispered, chasing away the dream of that faraway day.

Do you love me?

His heart thudded to a stop. The unspoken question hung in the air, as obvious as the barricade of a Halloween mask.

He couldn't bring himself to answer, to lie, to tell the truth. God, did he love her?

Of course not. He just wasn't capable. He'd only end up hurting her—and himself—in the end. And he'd been wounded too many times to expose himself to the need for love again.

He couldn't even bear to tell her his real plan for Spencer. What made him think he was worthy of love?

Instead of answering, he pulled her to the pillows on his bed, caressing some scarves from her skin, tentatively joining his throbbing lips to hers, coaxing the golden coins from her hair with infinite care. The shining pieces of metal clanged to the rug, muted thumps of treasure lost.

All but forgetting the pain in his lower lip, he kissed her thoroughly, on her soft mouth, behind her ear in that strawberry-scented cove, on the pulsing thrum of her neck, until she moaned low in her throat, trailing raspy scarves against his jeans with the stirrings of her body against his.

As always, she tasted like an ice-cream-slick fantasy, of summer fruit and spices warmed by the sun. Nick maneuvered her on top of him as he backed against the pillows. While she explored his chest with her fingertips, he slipped inside the veils, touching her flesh, hardening at her heat. She shifted over his excitement, urging him to cover her breasts with his palms.

Firm breasts, full as the sun warming his skin. He didn't know if he could take much more of this, day after day, wondering what would happen when his worst nightmare showed up in town.

"I love you so much," she said again, her voice strained by passion.

He couldn't answer with words, so he used his tongue to lightly stroke a desire-peaked nipple, bringing her to whimper, stoking her yearning until she cried out in fulfillment.

Two or three scarves fluttered over her body as she unbuttoned his pants and brought him to complete readiness with her hands and fingers. Then she took him into her warmth, swaying back and forth as he closed his eyes, held her hips, scratched the skin of her thighs.

She brought him to completeness, then gently brought him down amid an explosion, scattering the debris of his doubts all over his skin. The ashes of his climax sizzled, scarring him with guilt.

More scars.

Nick noticed the hot pink of Meggie's face, her agitation, so he guided her to her side and loved her until she clutched the headboard, loosened her grip and evened her breathing.

They cuddled in each other's arms, breathing together in a melancholy rhythm. "You're going to end up hating me," he murmured.

He only wished he could do something to stop the inevitable.

Chapter Fourteen

The next day Meg tripped around the bakery as if in a dream. Her nightmare about Jacob wasn't any less real, but she had Nick on her side now, helping her forgive herself for her part in the tragedy.

She was in love. And it felt great, a comforting balm to cushion the world's blows.

As Meg decorated the top of a cake with icing in the bakery's back room, Widow Antle, her newly hired help, ran the counter, attending to the customers. Allowing another person to help with the bakery was the only way Nick would agree to her working two days a week. But it was a small sacrifice for her sense of self-worth.

The front door bells jingled and, seconds later, Rachel stood in front of Meg, her friend's face flushed with what appeared to be anger.

"Can I talk with you?" Rachel asked.

Meg smiled, barely containing thoughts of her and Nick making love last night. "Shoot away."

"No, really, Meg. I'm serious here."

Rachel's green-gray eyes held more than anger, Meg realized. They seemed sad.

"Rachel, did something happen with your husband?"

"No, though I wish that were the case. Sit down." She took the icing bag from Meg and led her to a chair.

"Boy, I'm really getting the pregnant treatment," she joked, half hating to hear what Rachel had to say. She had a bad feeling it was about her.

Rachel sighed, took Meg's hands in hers. "I've been hearing rumors in town. Rumors about you and Nick."

Meg laughed. "Since when do you pay attention to the gossips?"

"I just want to make sure... I don't want you to be hurt, Meg."

Fear froze Meg solid. Every doubt she'd had about their marriage rushed back to her, drowning her in suspicion that had never left entirely. "Just tell me, Rachel."

"Okay. I'm just going to lay it out there. Folks have been saying that Nick married you to get back at Chad Spencer. Now, I don't know how they came up with this, but—"

"You know it's not true," interrupted Meg. Her heart wanted to punch its way out of her rib cage. "You know this town is full of mean, malicious, forked-tongued devils."

Rachel continued through this barrage. "Have you ever asked Nick?"

"Nick wants to protect my baby. You know that."

"Honey, don't take this the wrong way. But have

you ever thought about why Nick was so eager to marry you in the first place?''

Yes. Oh, yes, she'd thought about it. But she'd trusted him to do right by her, to erase the pain that Chad had caused before him.

Meg tried to smile, to pretend everything was as fine as it had been five minutes ago, before Rachel had made her privy to the town's gossip. ''It's just a case of bored people sticking their noses into places they don't belong, Rachel. Don't worry.''

She tried to tell herself the same.

But she did worry, all the way home, as Rachel drove her to the house on the hill. She worried all the way over to Nick's office. When she saw he wasn't there, she worried up the stairs, into his room, where she peeked out the open doors of his balcony. She could see his shadow perched on the widow's walk. She decided to trudge up the stairway to join him.

Gusts of a cold November wind greeted her, causing her to cross her arms protectively over her chest.

He seemed to be studying the gaslight-dim streets of Kane's Crossing, leaning on the wooden rail with a brooding ease. As she moved near, she paused to appreciate his chiseled profile, the dent in the chin she'd kissed, the wrinkles, near the one healthy eye, that had narrowed when she'd confessed her love last night.

He hadn't said anything in return, but she knew Nick didn't often prefer to communicate with words. Now, considering Rachel's piece of gossip, she wondered if there wasn't more to his silence.

What, was she crazy? Nick had married her to protect her family from Chad. And, after all, that made their marriage a business arrangement; she shouldn't assume that he returned her affections, even if his body had convinced her of it. She'd been the one dumb enough to fall in love during a marriage of convenience. What had he promised her besides protection for her child?

She padded over to him, pressing her breasts into the sinew of his back. Muscles bunched under her sensitive nipples, making them contract with longing. Her belly grooved into his firm backside, the material of her dress scratching against the denim.

"It's cold out here," she said.

A shudder traveled his length, and she wondered if his inner struggles frosted his attitude.

They stayed quiet, both to their own thoughts. Meg broke the tension.

"I need to ask you something, once and for all. And be absolutely truthful, okay?"

He didn't say anything, so she plunged on.

"I've just heard the strangest rumor, and…well, you know I'm not the most confident person in the world. I need to hear what you have to say, though. So don't hate me for asking."

Silence.

She took a breath, feeling as she had yesterday when she'd told him about Jacob. If Kane's Crossing could see how much he'd cared for her, holding her, making her guilt ebb away at a less threatening distance, they'd know about their marriage. How it was more than just business.

It had to be.

"They're saying that you married me to get back at Chad Spencer. But I know it's a bunch of hogwash." She laughed, expecting him to join in.

Nick stayed facing the town. "I didn't have a nightmare last night. Usually I do, every night. I remember what it was like to see Chaney's Drugstore explode. I remember Chad Spencer laughing his butt off while I was being shoved in the sheriff's car. I feel my skin being burned by cigarettes, and I see hate in the eyes of my new family. I loved my foster parents and worshipped my brother. I worshipped Sam. Do you know what it was like to realize they didn't want to see me again?''

He'd talked around an answer. It scared Meg. ''As you told me yesterday, those things are in the past, Nick. If I can forgive myself, you can forgive Chad. Can't you?''

He looked at her over his shoulder. A hard light blocked his eyes, a pale-blue screen that shut her out.

''Nick, I love you. We'll work this out.''

He turned back to watch the town. ''You don't know everything about me, Meggie. And until you do, I don't think you should shout your misguided sense of love from the rooftops.''

She thought about Chad and how he'd spat out his goodbye message before he'd left her house. Surely she meant more to Nick, *her husband,* than that. She'd taken a big chance with her heart by admitting her love; if he tossed her feelings aside, she'd never recover.

Cigarette burns, the truth about his real parents, the Spencer property sales... What could possibly be worse than those secrets? ''I'll put an ad in the *Kane's Crossing Gazette* announcing my love for you if I have to, Nick. It's taken me a long time to fall for someone, and I know I've found love with you.''

Her heart was jackhammering. She didn't know what she'd do if he told her he didn't—couldn't—love her.

Nick said, ''Let me explain something, and then decide. In the end, if you never want to see me again, I'll understand.''

He hadn't turned around to face her. That, and this great buildup of uncharacteristic speech, worried her, made her cross her arms even tighter. "Go on."

His voice was as low and cold. "I bought all those Spencer businesses, with the help of a friend who allowed my name to be kept out of it. I didn't want anyone to know who was taking over the town until it was done.''

"I pretty much knew that." Good, if that's all there was, she'd be relieved. She didn't approve of what he'd done, but it hadn't reflected on their marriage.

"That's not all."

Meg's throat swelled, choking her off from telling him to stop; she didn't want to hear any more.

Nick said, "I wanted to break the Spencers financially before I did it personally. At first I married you because I wanted Chad to know that his child was mine, and there was very little he could do about it."

"You didn't want to protect us?" she whispered.

"Honestly, part of me did, just like I was helping out those poor families who got their homes taken away by the Spencers."

"So I was a charity case. Poor Meg, gone and got herself preggers and can't fend for herself.''

Obviously he had no words to defend himself, judging by his lack of them.

"So what was the big plan?" she asked, her voice gaining in strength.

His back stiffened. "I had a detective look into Chad's fiancée's background. She's rich, and I have no doubt Spencer's marrying her for the money. I even thought of letting him and his fiancée know about your baby's parentage, just to see if she'd drop him cold. At least, I was hoping that would be the result.''

Her words cracked with shock at the scope of his revenge plan. ''But they say she's barren, and if you're wrong about her leaving him, they could go after my child if they knew it was his.'' Meg shook with fury, her stomach muscles jumping. She hoped to God she wasn't upsetting the baby. ''I thought... I thought marrying you would keep him out of my life, but it's just reeled him farther in, hasn't it?''

He didn't move, silent and rigid as stone.

''And I told you all about my worries. You encouraged me to marry you, dammit! Do you have any conscience whatsoever?''

He turned around, eyes throwing flames the color of sun flares. The world seemed to stop around him, freezing into cold cruelty. ''Problem is, I have too much of a conscience, one that nags at me to pay back Chad for everything he's done to everybody in this town.''

''Don't you dare justify yourself, Nick Cassidy. I only hope the Renos aren't looking down from heaven to see what you've become.''

It was a low blow, and she knew it. She wanted to strike out at him, to knock him to his knees in agony. She wanted his motions to mirror the chaos inside her soul. ''I trusted you. I ripped my ugliest moment from my memories yesterday, and you pretended to care.''

''I do care.'' He took a step forward, holding out a hand to her. ''More than you'll ever know.''

''Liar. You don't care about me or this child. You manipulated my trust in you. You used me to bring another man down. How do you think that makes me feel?'' She backed away, trying to calm herself.

''You care, all right, Nick Cassidy. You care about

ruining Chad Spencer for a stupid teenage prank. It was a mean joke, that's for sure, but it happened sixteen years ago.''

He tugged down the line of his jeans, not because he was hooking his thumbs into the loops as a careless gesture, but because he wanted to remind her of those steaming, red scars he'd received after Chad's ''joke.'' It occurred to Meg that his I-don't-really-give-a-fig stance was actually a mask between the world and his old wounds. And she was probably the only one who knew.

One of the burns seemed to throb in the moonlight. ''*This* happened after the prank,'' he said. He pointed to another one. ''And this, and…''

''I've got the message.'' Her voice grated. ''Tell me. Are you out for justice or revenge? Because there is a difference, you know.''

His arms curved slightly at his sides in a defensive posture. ''I'm not about to wait for fate, or whatever it is that controls our punishments, to take care of my business.''

''That's the way life works, Nick. Why can't you understand?'' Her throat burned, cutting off words. When she recovered, she tried again. ''What comes around goes around. It's not up to you to force the outcome.''

''You know I can't agree with that.''

She thought of his car crash, edging him to the precipice of death. ''It's just not the way I'd handle things.''

Wind blew between them, providing a chilly wall.

''So is my baby just another corporate takeover for you? Was betraying me and this child worth all your hard work, Nick?'' Meg cleared her throat, fearing that her anger would give out on her, keep her from telling him just how much she hurt inside. "You know, yesterday, after I told you about Jacob, I thought I'd never feel wounded again. What you've done to me is a million times worse."

His form remained rocky, but she sensed something melt within him. Maybe it was the set of his shoulders that dropped a little. Maybe it was the firm line of his mouth. Or the way his swelled eye softened his expression.

He said, "You're right about some of it. I started out thinking of your child as a tool to hurt Spencer. But that all changed, Meggie."

This childhood pet name made her cringe. "Stop calling me that."

She'd punctured him, making his gaze lower, making him step farther away. Too late. She couldn't take it back. Neither of them could erase these past couple of months—or what had come before.

His voice floated on the breeze. "Please consider this. We'll buy a house in whatever state you want. You can raise the baby there under another name—"

"So you can tell Chad the child is his? So you can get the satisfaction of turning his wife against him?"

"Be reasonable."

She could see that he'd clenched his jaw, his fists. He was a time bomb ready to explode. "None of this is reasonable. I feel for the hurting boy inside you, I really do, but..."

"I don't need your pity."

"No." Hot tears washed over her face, but she held her head up with dignity. "You just don't need *me*."

"Meggie..."

She started to walk away from him, afraid that her

anger would only grow if she stayed. "If revenge is a dish best served cold, then you can be sure that it'll make a pretty lousy partner in bed."

She almost gasped at the venom in her words. Nick merely turned around again, facing Kane's Crossing. It was appropriate, since that was his first love anyway.

"One question," she said, before leaving entirely.

He didn't move.

She didn't care. "Would you have been willing to accept Chad's child as your own?"

Meg had a pretty good idea by now that when Nick chose to hold back in silence, there was a reason. His lack of response told her everything she needed to know.

"It doesn't matter," she said. "Even if I have to live the rest of my life alone, I'll make it without your help."

She waited for him to say something. Anything. He was breaking her heart all over again and, oddly enough, she hadn't fallen to pieces, she hadn't dissolved into nothing. She'd make it, dammit. Her *and* her child.

She continued. "By morning, I want you out of my house. Out of Kane's Crossing. You do what you need to do with Chad, but be aware that I'll fight both of you along the way."

Her heartbeats punctuated the air, and still, no response.

Meg shook her head, grinding her teeth. How had she been foolish enough to get her soul torn in two by yet another man? One thing was for certain—it'd never happen again.

Never.

Images of Nick standing up for her in the bakery and

at the Halloween dance zoomed across her mind's eye. His leathery scent, the bulk of his arms, his hand balling her stomach as he talked with her baby…

She'd whispered, "You didn't learn a damned thing, did you?" Then she'd left.

Now, huddled, tearless, on her bed, she waited for him to pack his duffel bag and leave her forever.

She couldn't even take pride in the fact that she'd stood up for herself, just like she used to do before life had beat her down.

She couldn't even appreciate Nick's hand in giving her back some of that old confidence.

Meg felt as lost as the day she'd been kicked out of San Diego. Lost and devoid of hope.

Nick would've given his fortune to have been able to answer Meggie when she'd asked about accepting Chad's baby as his own. But he'd been so overcome with emotion, he thought he'd make an *idiot* out of himself by breaking down, kneeling at her feet, begging her to understand his dilemma.

Be seen and not heard.

It'd finally been his downfall.

And it was too late to apologize to Meggie. What was there left to explain? Now that all his secrets were out in the open, she still hated him, and for good reason. He couldn't even stand himself.

But he had a quest to complete, because no one else would do it for him. He needed to restore his pride, polish the memories of his foster family and come to the aid of the people who'd been victimized by Chad Spencer for too long.

He packed his lone bag, just as he'd done when he'd

been moved from each foster home. He walked out Meggie's door for the last time.

A puff of magnolia scent escorted him out and, as he started down the hill, the house towering above him like a crow's wing, he thought he heard weeping in the cry of the bird circling above his head.

He thought of the cradle he'd never put in the renovated nursery, and almost trooped back to get it. Then sanity grabbed at his throat, leading him to the garage for his pickup.

She'd never take him back. Not after his words—or lack of them—had bruised her like well-aimed stones.

As he drove through the deserted streets of Kane's Crossing, a torn Welcome Home, Chad banner waved goodbye, clapping in the wind.

Chapter Fifteen

Three months later, in the throes of the February doldrums, Meg rested in a padded chair in the old house's completed nursery. Bright layers of pink, blue and lavender complemented the cuddly pictures of kitties and puppies that decorated the comforters, quilted wall-hangings and striped curtains.

She was a whale, feeling as if she'd swallowed a beach ball that had been slowly inflating for nine long months. It seemed as if the extra weight gain filled the places Nick had left empty. More frequently now, she'd feel a squirming in her belly, as if the life inside was caught in a space too small. Or as if it was punishing Meg for allowing Nick to leave.

What would he have done if he'd been around long enough to find out she was carrying twins? Would he have pressed his ear to her stomach to hear their dual heartbeats? Would he have conversed with them in his soothing, low voice, making her breath catch in her throat?

There she went again. Every day she promised herself she wouldn't think about her estranged husband, wouldn't wonder where he was or if he was thinking about her, as well. About two months ago she'd received a letter from him, and she wondered if it contained divorce papers, but she hadn't bothered to open it; she didn't want to be reminded of his justifications and more lies. Nobody would betray her again.

Then another packet had arrived. And another. All unopened, waiting patiently in a kitchen drawer.

Meg had even avoided answering the phone, allowing her archaic answering machine to pick up the calls. Several times a week, she'd hear the tentative click of a hang-up when the caller realized she wasn't about to respond.

She'd told Nick that she could make it on her own, and she meant it—even if feeding twins would stretch her limited income even more than she'd first planned. Sometimes Meg sat up late at night, adding numbers, trying to figure out how her new family would get by.

She had a feeling the letters Nick had sent contained checks. But she'd be damned if she cashed them.

In the meantime, she'd counted on Widow Antle to work in the bakery, and Meg would drop in for an hour or two each day, sitting in a comfortable chair in the back room, keeping up the stock of "magical" blueberry pies and angel food cakes.

Yes, she'd make it on her own.

Nick's cradle loomed in the corner of the nursery. She'd toyed with the idea of throwing it away, but, just as Aunt Valentine had cherished and sworn loyalty to this old house, Meg felt a connection with the old-fashioned object. Besides, on the practical side, she needed to buy another one for the twin, and she couldn't afford two.

Rachel Shane strolled into the room, took one gander at Meg's wilted posture and assumed the worst. "Are you still stressing out about the money? I told you, I'll help you."

"No. You'll be paying that detective to find your husband until Judgment Day. Besides, I'm doing fine."

Rachel chuffed. "I wonder if my trusty Sherlock Holmes gives two-for-one offers. You know, a deserted wife special."

Meg's heart fisted, and her friend came to the chair to hug her.

"Sorry. That was uncalled for," she said.

"Things can only get better." Meg tried to smile, but she'd lost practice, and her muscles strained to complete the simple task.

Rachel put a hand on her shoulder. "Are you ready to go?"

Meg sighed. Today marked the time Chad would return to town. Kane's Crossing, welcoming back the football hero from his far-off journeys. His train was due within the hour.

She could see it now. The ladies' auxiliary was planning a victory walk down Main Street, in spite of the recent foul weather that had left the road lined with slush. The good citizens of the town would decorate the sidewalks, waving, kissing up to the financial god of the county so he wouldn't punish them for straying from the path by embracing Nick Cassidy during the stranger's short stay.

At least, that's how Deacon Chaney had put it. Word in town was that the Spencer family was making a strong bid to repurchase their property—the Mercantile, the bank, the market, the hardware store, the toy factory. They'd even been bragging about buying Nick's abandoned shopping arcade by Cutter's Lake.

Her husband had disappeared as quietly as mist over the moon, leaving the town vulnerable once again. Meg's soul keened over Nick's loss of spirit, and her part in driving him away. It hurt even more to hear the gossip in the bakery—the bitter words about how he'd deserted them.

Nick had lifted the town up and removed the bottom from their lives, leaving them to fall to earth with a deafening crash.

Even the displaced families who'd moved back into their houses were running scared, worried that Chad was going to kick them out again. A few hadn't even bothered to move back into their newly refurbished homes.

As Meg slowly rose from her chair, she thought she heard a low whistle in the distance.

Chad was nearing Kane's Crossing.

Rachel rushed out of the room, pausing long enough to toss a comment over her shoulder. "That's the teapot screaming at me. We have enough time for a cup, then we need to leave if you're going to go through with this harebrained scheme of yours."

Meg flinched, remembering Nick's own plan. Had she become what she'd accused him of being? A vigilante who had decided to punish according to a misguided code of honor?

Not even close.

Nick had shown her that anger wasn't the best tool for revenge. But she'd darn well go to her problem before it came to her.

He'd at least taught her that much.

After they drank their tea, Rachel drove Meg to town, their rattle-plagued little car traveling under the weight of livid, gunmetal-hued clouds, threatening to rain bullets.

Rachel pulled an angora scarf around her throat. "I can't believe you're out here in the cold, Meg. You should be resting at home. This is only adding to your anxiety."

Meg huddled next to her friend, peeking through two old men blowing puffs of cold air from their mouths. They were facing Main Street, waiting for Chad and his fiancée to stroll out of their Lexus and into the pet grooming shop—the only property the Spencers still officially owned. She had to admit, seeing the expression on his face as he sashayed into his family's remaining enterprise might be fairly amusing.

"Rachel, stop fretting. You bundled me up in these layers of material. I look like the poor actors who had to wear Ewok costumes in *Return of the Jedi*."

"I still register my protest vote." Rachel craned her neck as a tinny strain of recorded music broke the chilly air. "You've got to be kidding. They're playing a cotton-picking, Fourth-of-July-celebrating, red-white-and-blue, goose-stepping march, for heaven's sake. This is too much."

Meg's blood began to boil. Now she *really* wanted to confront Chad, to fire a preemptory missile at him, letting him know that these babies had nothing to do with him.

It was a desperate move, but she couldn't think of any other way around it. Meg was going to lie, just as

Nick had lied to her. She was going to tell Chad that the babies weren't his.

She despised herself, but she couldn't think of a better way to keep her children.

Temperance, she thought. She needed to keep her wits about her, to calmly take the situation in hand without losing control of her emotions.

Nick had taught her well. Too bad he couldn't have learned the same, because he might've been around to welcome her twins into the world.

And, in the dark of the night, when she lay in bed, missing the touch of his warm, bare skin, she couldn't help hating herself for driving him away, for withholding forgiveness as her parents had done to her.

She cleared her throat to dispel the sadness that was blocking her air passage. Nick wouldn't be returning. She'd made sure of that with her fear and stubbornness.

A crowd appeared, strutting down the street as if they owned it. And they almost did.

Members of the ladies' auxiliary were dressed in their finest, tossing brightly wrapped candy to people who'd stepped out of shops to see what the commotion was all about. High school cheerleaders had dressed in their tight sweaters, clutching the arms of varsity football and basketball players. The proceeding seemed more like a homecoming parade more than anything else.

Gary Joanson approached, holding a boom box that was belting out the march. Meg caught his eye, and his gaze zipped away. He stumbled as he passed.

His wife followed, staring at Meg, her stomach swollen with child.

Heck, Meg thought. The woman couldn't even be grateful for Meg's magical chocolate baby cake. In

Kane's Crossing, true respect came at a much higher price.

Rachel leaned over to mutter in Meg's ear. "I'm waiting for *The X-Files* crew to show up."

Meg didn't respond. She could sense Chad coming nearer. She knew this because the hairs on the back of her neck were standing on edge, like an animal sensing danger.

A blond head stood above the rest of the crowd. The coppery-blood taste of terror lingered in her mouth.

Suddenly, someone dressed in a pink sweat suit with the hood pulled over their head darted into the street. As everyone else watched the procession, Meg saw the figure drop a paper bag in Chad's path, then disappear.

Distracted for merely a moment, Meg returned her attention back to her ex…whatever he was.

Chad seemed cockier than ever, strutting at a purposeful clip, not seeming to care at all that Nick had almost ruined his livelihood. It made her ill to think that he'd underestimate her husband, even if she didn't agree with Nick's methods. She wished the man she loved could've come out a winner.

Her vision seemed to focus into one pinpoint of light as Chad's royal-blue eyes met hers. His smile dimmed for an instant before it wrenched back into an arrogant curve.

At that moment she knew that he knew what everyone had been saying about the father of her child. She held back the sinking feeling that he'd go after the babies.

The object that had been placed in the street by the stealthy pink sweatshirt caused Chad to trip. He stopped, lifted up his Italian-leather loafer and cursed out loud.

Rachel's hearty laugh shot through the cold. Meg took a step away from her, distancing herself. This wasn't a time to cheer.

"Phew," said Rachel, "someone took a bagful of souvenirs from the horse farm."

Chad's voice grated over the music. "Ashlyn!"

An amused voice rang out. "Welcome home, Chad!"

Ashlyn Spencer, hood down, stood behind Meg and Rachel, waved, then darted in the opposite direction. Sheriff Carson hefted his girth as he passed by them in a poor imitation of a chase.

Chad grabbed the hand of the lovely woman next to him, leading her into the Perky Puppies Dog Grooming Shop.

The fiancée. The woman who very well might want to take her children from her.

It was time for Meg to settle her own score.

She waited by the grooming shop's crepe-lined window, staring at two tail-wagging Maltese dogs with ribbons in their hair, keeping her eye on Chad until the well-wishers finished paying court to the returning prince. He stepped out the front door of the shop, and she took up his trail.

He came to rest against the building's brick facade, propping a cleaned loafer against the wall, nipping a cigarette from a golden package and leaning back his blond head. Cupping his hand to light the tip, he sucked in a drag, closing his eyes in apparent ecstasy.

Meg shivered, not only because his expression reminded her of their almost-regretful night together, but because of the circular glow-burn. She thought of

Nick's wounds, the red welts forever crisped to his skin.

The man who'd just about singed her husband was in front of her now, James Dean-ing against the wall as if he alone suffered all the troubles the world had to offer.

Prankster or monster? Meg had a good idea which name she preferred. As she studied his pretty-boy profile, she wondered what she'd ever seen in him.

Neatly clipped hair the color of sun shining on a pile of coins, cool-blue eyes that seemed to hold his many fans in thrall, a jawline that even Rob Lowe would envy.

That's right. Every girl's dream.

Her sturdy brown boots made a wincing sound in the slush as she walked to his side.

It wasn't too late. She could turn around now and run away to another state, another town, as Nick had wanted her to.

That's crazy, she told herself. *If you flee now, you'll be fleeing for all time.*

Meg waited for Chad to notice her presence, half hoping her coat hid her belly. Fat chance.

After an eternity of heartbeats, he finally came up for another long cigarette fix. His frosty eyes scanned her from head to heel. "What?"

After everything she'd been through, all he had to say was "What?" She wanted to sneer and walk away, but that'd defeat the purpose of this premeditated face-off.

She said, "Congratulations on your engagement," keeping the venom from her tone quite successfully. Pity she couldn't say the same for her trembling falsetto.

Chad narrowed his gaze, then, after a moment, blew a bitter stream of smoke in her face.

Meg backed away, cursing herself for getting too close in the first place. If she'd been thinking about the babies, she'd have realized that they wouldn't benefit from lungfuls of carcinogens.

He flicked some ash onto the mud-specked ground. "Still living in that Addams Family mansion?"

She nodded.

"Interesting." Chad grinned at Sonny, Junior and Gary Joanson, who'd joined their cozy group.

Wonderful. Now what would she do?

Sonny bummed a cigarette from the leader of the pack while Chad said, "We're buying your place, you know. Dad always wanted to tear down that eyesore. He says it's a pox on the town's beautiful face."

To cry out in surprise would've thrilled Chad, so she kept her emotions in check. Even if she wanted to get down on her knees and beg mercy for Aunt Valentine's treasured family landmark, Meg wouldn't do it.

"Over my dead body," she said.

The men chuckled. All except Gary, who'd come to stand just in front of Meg. Not that she felt protected in any way by the little man, but she was faintly grateful for his support.

"Chad, I wonder if we could talk in private," she said.

He spread his hands in a careless gesture. "What's the difference? These boys keep no secrets from me, and vice versa."

His meaning wasn't lost on her. His "boys" had told Chad everything he needed to know about the past months and Nick's part in them.

All right then. They'd play this game on his terms,

but she'd still come out the victor. "Then you know I'm going to have twins."

She left the rest of the tale hanging in the late winter air, sharp as hardened snow. Meg could hear people breathing behind her, and she glanced over her shoulder.

A crowd had formed, pulled out of the grooming shop by the lack of Chad's presence, no doubt. Ashlyn lingered on the fringes, watching her brother, her ever-present, impish grin straightened by the weight of Meg's comment. Deacon Chaney and Rachel were walking across the street, curious expressions on their faces. The fiancée broke through the bodies to stand by Chad's side, peering up at him from beneath her stylish purple cap.

Heck, Meg could never take the easy way out. Either she could wait for Chad to respond, or she could take matters into her own hands.

But the fiancée beat her to the punch. "What is going on, Chad?"

She sounded so sweet, so sincere with her little Euro accent, that Meg almost hated to involve her.

Chad ground out the cigarette beneath his heel. "Sweetie, I've got nothing to do with—"

A low, gravely voice roughened the atmosphere, turning heads and halting movement as efficiently as a roll of thunder.

"You sure as hell do."

Meg's world stopped spinning and, as she turned to face the stranger, her sight dimmed, her body hummed.

Nick. Poised in gunfighter stance, dressed in darkness from his leather jacket to the toe of his boots. Lines around his frown spoke of cloud-filled nights. Angry red abrasions on his knuckles attested to more bouts with shattered windows or noses. Most frightening of all were his eyes, chilled with nursed hatred and the cold fire of revenge.

Her heart swelled with the memory of music, starlight and long nights of lovemaking. Then it bled with sorrow, every drop a lost hope.

After all, he'd returned to finish his business. It had nothing to do with her and the babies. And now she didn't even have the option of lying to Chad, telling him that Nick was the babies' father.

She'd been backed into a corner.

Chad's face lit up, much as it always had when he was a fourteen-year-old and he'd seen Nick approaching his posse. "Well, look what the cat dragged out from juvie. If it isn't Nick Cassidy. I hear you've been busy."

Nick hadn't even glanced at her. Meg wanted to sink to the ground to fade with the slush, erasing her presence.

He was here to complete his revenge. Somehow, he'd lost his iron hold on his plan to financially ruin Chad. Now he was here to decimate his nemesis personally by revealing her secrets to him and driving Chad's fiancée away.

So why couldn't she bring herself to hate him? Why did she want to run into his arms and kiss him until he melted into her?

Damn him for leaving. Damn her for forcing him to go.

Nick hadn't answered Chad's taunt. He merely stared at him, Deacon and Rachel flanking his back. Her friend shot Meg a worried glance, but Meg shook her head, silently telling Rachel she could handle whatever happened.

Because no one—absolutely no one—was going to threaten her children. She'd die before that happened.

She only wished the man she loved felt the same way.

Pushing off from the wall, Chad stood straighter, Sonny and Junior stationed by his sides like rusty six-shooters. "I hear you've done pretty well for yourself, probably by dishonest means, knowing you. But what it boils down to is, you can't come into Kane's Crossing and throw around your money."

A disbelieving laugh echoed over the tension. Ashlyn yelled, "Look who's talking, Chad." Several people shuffled their feet. Sheriff Carson huffed into view again, and Ashlyn took to her heels.

Chad stuck his finger in his sister's direction. "I'll deal with you at home!" His pointed appendage wavered to Nick. "Listen, you might think you own this town, but we're in the process of acquiring all the property you stole from my family."

Meg couldn't stay quiet any longer. "Stole?"

"Meggie." Nick had said her name, but he still hadn't looked her way.

Why couldn't she bring herself to leave? If she was smart, she'd run away now. Away from Chad. Away from the man who'd returned to complete his plan for justice.

But she couldn't tear herself away from his steely glare, away from his most important stand in Kane's Crossing.

Chad continued, his words whizzing by with the speed of bullets. "I've come home to drive evil out of this town. Jobs will be plentiful, and nobody will ever have to worry about losing their livelihoods to a corporate demon."

An ironic smile scythed Nick's lips, but he didn't say a word. Inwardly, Meg urged him on. Now wasn't the time to stay silent. Now was the time to speak up, to defend himself.

Forget everything your real father ever screamed at you. Say something!

Without thinking, she backed away from the line of fire, realizing, too late, that she'd come to stand next to the fiancée. They shadowed each other, glanced warily, then broke eye contact.

Chad was going to ruin another life. Too bad this woman didn't know it yet.

The crowd was listening in rapt attention. Nick stood amid the townsfolk, almost as if he was one of them.

In reaction to Nick's silence, Chad's ire had risen, mottling his cheeks to a most unroyal shade of crimson. "What's got your tongue, Cassidy? Even *I* thought you'd learn to enunciate in sixteen years. Didn't they have correspondence courses in juvie?"

Silence. But Meg could see Nick's jaw muscles working. She wondered if he was remembering the explosion, the sheriff's car taking him away from his foster family. She wanted to stand by his side, to make a show of unity, except...

They weren't united.

If she knew Nick as well as she thought she did, he'd be restraining his temper, holding back his itching trigger finger.

Meg didn't know how long her secrets would stay locked in his mind. With every insult, Chad poked a sleeping monster. A monster Chad hadn't realized he'd created when he'd framed Nick Cassidy the night of the bombing.

Chad obviously couldn't resist one last shot. "Awwww. Does the mute Salvation Army clotheshorse have hurt feelings? Maybe Mommy and Daddy can kiss it better.''

Nick flinched, bucking back as if struck by cold lead.

Meg knew Chad had gone too far, stirring the ashes of sacred memories that featured a loving foster family.

Even the faces of the town's citizens reflected disgust at how far their golden boy had stooped. Several supporters who'd been attempting to get back into Chad's good graces in the grooming shop backed away from their former football hero. Gary Joanson took Meg's hand, guiding her to stand near Nick.

Sonny and Junior even seemed a tad repulsed.

When the Spencer Factory had experienced the accident that had killed Nick's foster dad plus ten others, it'd saddened the whole town. Chad's knock had obviously opened some old wounds.

And still, Nick stood his ground. He could've lashed out in a blind rage. He could've used his own words to cat-o'-nine-tails Chad.

But he waited, a man of honor. Even if Meg knew he was hiding a gaping wound in his soul.

She couldn't help admiring him. Loving him.

But would he let her down?

A bead of sweat trembled on Chad's upper lip. His fiancée had faded behind him, eyes wide as she scanned the citizens' faces.

Slowly, Chad turned his attention to Meg and trailed his gaze over her stomach, her breasts. She protectively crossed her arms.

''So you're married now,'' said Chad, changing tack. ''Hell of a shotgun wedding. I wonder why that is.''

Meg's palms slid down to her stomach. This was the

moment she'd been waiting for, a chance to clear the air and make her intentions known so she'd never have to worry again.

Except Nick wasn't really the father, and she had no one else to claim her babies.

"Oh," continued Chad. "But then there was that nasty breakup. Could it be that there's trouble in paradise?"

Meg held her breath, waiting for Nick to lash out with the truth—that he'd merely married her for revenge's sake.

The wind howled softly. The town church bell tolled the hour. One…two…three…four…

Chad smiled grimly, his eyes peeling away Meg's clothing, layer by layer.

…Five…six…seven…eight…

Meg stepped to Nick's side, looking up at him. He watched her with cool-blue indifference, but below the surface she could sense a current of something else, something powerful.

…Nine…ten…eleven…

Chad chuckled. "You have to love a marriage between a criminal and the town whore."

…Twelve.

Nick's leather jacket creaked as he tensed and shifted. When he finally spoke, he didn't use his words to defend himself. And they didn't condemn her.

His voice balanced on the thin edge of a blade as he stared at his lifelong enemy. "I'm here to take my wife and my children home. Meggie?"

Relief almost sagged her to her knees. A cry welled up in her throat, threatening to blind her with tears. But how could he want to take her home after she'd kicked him out of it? Was he merely "saving" her again, protecting her from Chad?

Nick took her hands in his, heat zapping through her skin, his calluses feeling like a touch of home-worn comfort. His voice shook through the air. "I love you, Meggie. Are you coming with me?"

Love. He'd said love. Her heart soared, but she still didn't understand.

Chad's cruel laughter brought Meg back to the moment.

"Yeah, right," he said. "We're supposed to believe that you've come back to Kane's Crossing for Witchy Poo."

Meg tried to shut him out of her mind. Was Nick just attempting to rile Chad with his proclamation of love? She stared into his eyes, seeking confirmation of his feelings.

And she found it. A softening in his gaze, the pressure of his thumb gliding over hers. *He loved her.*

But she still wasn't sure she'd give him a chance to hurt her again.

Meg turned to Chad, willing to follow Nick's lead to save her babies. "He's the father of my children. Why wouldn't he come back?"

Chad smirked. "Because he wants to snake my businesses away from me again. Well, too bad, Cassidy. We're going to own what's ours."

Nick kept a hold of Meg's hand, offering her a reassuring smile. Then he aimed a glare at Chad. "I'm afraid you're mistaken, Spencer. If you want to buy the properties back, you're going to have to deal with someone else. I don't own them anymore."

Chad raised his eyebrow. "What the hell are you talking about?"

Nick shrugged. "Remember those families you drove out of town? The ones whose houses you took over for the land? Talk business with them. They own everything you used to, except the bank. Talk to my friends at Walters and Friedel, Incorporated, about that."

In the background, Deacon Chaney clapped his hands and let out a bellow. Several more citizens joined in.

"And," Nick continued, "don't expect to collect interest on any more loans. I've paid off every single one of them. You don't control anyone in Kane's Crossing anymore."

Over the crowd's gasps of astonishment, Nick shook his head. "Months ago, I came back to town to make your life hell. But you pretty much took care of getting there yourself."

Chad's grimace accelerated Meg's worries. She knew he wasn't above totally ruining Nick's life. His teenage bomb prank had established that much.

He surveyed the crowd, probably assessing who was still on his side. And, judging by the smug stares, she guessed the number wasn't very high. Meg noticed that he avoided the increasingly curious gaze of his fiancée. She waited for him to cover his embarrassment by shifting the attention to someone else, namely them.

He didn't disappoint. "There he goes, ladies and gentlemen, lying again. You can't trust someone who tried to blow up the town."

Gary Joanson stepped up next to Nick, his bantam stance dwarfed by her husband's stature. "Shut up, Chad. Everyone knows you did it. You're the one who should've been in the sheriff's car and kicked out of town."

Chad glared. "You're scum, Joanson."

Deacon Chaney's voice rang out. "And you're slime-licking scum, Chad Spencer!"

This time, voices rose in agreement, heavy as a soul-cleansing rainfall. The crowd started to break up as people swamped Nick and Meg, wanting to shake her husband's hand or to thump him on the back in appreciation.

Meg caught her breath, covering her stomach as she slid out of the throng of people. Nick's gaze connected with hers, promising that this wasn't over.

What was she going to say to him? What could she do?

Suddenly, Chad was in her face. "I could ruin your marriage with a few words, Meg. Who says I don't have any more control?"

She started to tremble, heart-jigging waves of fear washing over her.

Then Nick was at her side again, his arm supporting her. "You have something more to say?"

"Yeah," Chad said. "I just want you to know that I slept with your wife. And she screamed with pure joy the whole time I gave it to her."

Nick's fists bunched the back of her jacket. Images of a punched car window shattered her confidence in him.

Please, she thought, *don't fall into his trap.*

His grip loosened. "Good try, Spencer. But I'm the one who's going to love her for the rest of our lives."

Sadness tugged at her. She didn't know if she could let him back into her life. It had hurt too much last time.

Out of the corner of her eye, she caught sight of

Chad's fiancée, noticing something she hadn't before. The pooch of her poncho, her thickened waistline.

As Meg's eyes widened, Nick pulled her away from Chad. The golden boy screamed obscenities at them, then reversed colors and began shouting promises to the dispersing crowd. They waved him off, leaving only a few to linger by his side. Ashlyn Spencer was one of them, as was his fiancée.

In silence, Nick loaded Meg into his truck. The splash of tires running through the wet roads was the only conversation as he drove to her house.

He pulled into the driveway, and she opened her own door before he could get out of the cab. She halted his movement by laying a hand on his jacket.

His blue eyes held all the hope of a war-wounded stare. Apparently, he knew that she wouldn't take him back, that he'd never had a chance after setting his revenge plan into motion.

Her sigh was a jagged one. "Thanks for the ride."

As she started to leave the vehicle, he whispered, "Meggie?"

Plaintive. Yearning. The tone of a hurt animal scratching at a door, wanting to come inside. He almost had her, but Meg was terrified to give in to his unspoken plea.

Once bitten, twice shy. She couldn't get over the fear of Nick hurting her again. The niggling doubts that he'd betrayed her once and could do it again still remained.

Was he holding back more secrets? Would he change his mind and bring Chad Spencer down even lower?

She couldn't risk it. Her babies needed a stable father. She wasn't even sure he truly loved her; the word might've just been a tool to anger Chad.

She left the pickup, afraid to answer him.

Afraid to look back.

Chapter Sixteen

The following week had been filled with exhausting, backyard-renovating work for Nick. But winning Meggie back would be worth every minute.

He leaned back on his haunches, slipped his hammer into the loop of his jeans and grabbed a bandanna from his back pocket to wipe his forehead. Sweat had soaked through his T-shirt and two flannel shirts, making his stomach shiver deep inside, even if it was an unseasonably warm late February afternoon.

From his view on the roof of the old servants' quarters where he was nailing shingles, he peered at the stately house, hoping to see a sign of Meggie and a too-big-to-believe stomach. Wishing she'd step outside to talk to him.

But, over the course of these seven days, she hadn't even said hello.

During Nick's absence, he'd kept in contact with

Deacon and Rachel, living Meggie's life with her through endless questions and descriptions of how big she was getting, of how she was expecting twins, of how sad her eyes seemed. Out of desperation, he'd tried to call a time or two, yet she'd never answered. And leaving a message on the machine was never an option. He'd sent letters, the words torn from the agony he felt at leaving her, but those, too, hadn't gotten a response. She hadn't even cashed his checks.

Convinced that she still hated him, Nick had decided to search for Sam Reno, his foster brother. If anything good had come out of his separation from Meggie, it'd been his time with Sam. Even though Sam was undergoing tough times, they'd bonded again, feeling like brothers once more.

Nick had found Sam in Washington, D.C., a broken-spirited man in the wake of his wife's recent death. The rumors had been true; he'd dropped out of the police force, leaving himself with nothing but time on his hands.

Nick's heart ached for his older brother, the agony in Sam's lifeless gaze. He wanted to bring back the guy who'd loved drag racing on the back roads of Kane's Crossing, the guy who'd always introduced Nick as his real brother—even though they knew it wasn't a legal fact.

In D.C., they'd watched hockey games and talked over too many beers. They'd cleared up the past and promised to keep in touch. It was all Nick could've hoped for.

Then, Nick had searched his soul, wondering how Meggie would ever forgive him for his arrogance and stupidity. Wondering what it would take to make her love him again.

He'd returned to his corporate offices, tried wearing a tie, but that had failed miserably. His days were empty without the feel of Meggie's stomach in his palm, the glow of her smile warming his heart.

The day Deacon Chaney phoned changed everything. Chad Spencer was coming back to town.

Nick knew Meggie would need him more than ever, so, whether or not she'd welcome him back, he returned to Kane's Crossing to take his chances.

He'd almost lost his temper while facing Spencer in the street. But Meggie had taught him a lesson or two about controlling himself, and about forgiveness. Not that he held any soft place in his heart for Spencer, but he did kind of feel sorry for him.

At least the jerk was back in Europe, chasing around his fiancée. She'd left him the day of the confrontation, causing the golden boy to desert the family businesses. Nick didn't know if this meant Spencer was in love or not, but he decided to believe the best.

Yeah, his attitude was surprising, but fair. Especially since Nick felt such relief at hearing the gossips had been mistaken about the fiancée's barren state. Spencer just might've gone off to chase his legacy—his son or daughter. Hopefully, this meant he'd never concern himself with Meggie again.

Oddly enough, he felt no sense of victory, no explosive thrust of poetic justice. Life was nothing without Meggie.

Nick sat up straighter as the nursery's pastel curtains parted just enough to allow him a heart-wrenching peek of curly red hair.

Come out, he thought, wishing he could explain so much to her. But he wouldn't push it. She needed time, just as he'd needed it.

He sighed. The Mercantile had delivered a bassinet to the house today, the one Meggie had wanted when they'd shopped for baby items. He knew she needed two, now that she was carrying twins. He wished he could see the nursery, himself.

Nick smiled, hefting the hammer to his fist again. Twins. He couldn't understand why he felt doubly proud; he wasn't really the father. Meggie was making damned sure he knew it, too.

Trouble was, he'd gotten pretty used to the fact that Spencer was the father. He'd accepted their paternity, knowing long ago that they had no part in it. Just as he'd had no part in his own choice of parents.

Below, the kitchen door tapped against the frame, and his head shot up. Meggie stood on the deadened grass, craning her neck to see him as she massaged her back. She seemed so vulnerable with her incredibly huge belly that Nick's heart twisted.

She held up a batch of paper. His opened letters. "I guess I should thank you."

"For what?" Should he stay cool and calm, or scoot right down there to wrap her in his arms?

"For the words." She blushed. "I know how hard it is for you to say what matters."

His pulse pounded. "Like 'I love you'?"

Sigh. "I can't believe you haven't given up yet. A whole week out here, waiting for something to happen. What did you think I'd do? Forget everything and welcome you back?"

He drove a nail into a shingle. The urge to stay silent overwhelmed him, but he knew Meggie needed to hear what he'd returned to say. "I was hoping as much. And I'll find as many home improvements as I need to get you to sit down and talk things out."

Bang! Another nail.

"I still don't understand why you came back to a town that looked down on you for so long. How could you?"

He held the hammer silent, locking gazes with hers. Her beautiful green eyes glanced longingly at him, giving him hope. He knew what he wanted to say, but the words were heavy. Finally he forced them out. "Because *you're* my home, my heart. I go where you go."

She bit her lip, shut her eyes, then turned to leave. If he'd been flying high at her willingness to talk with him, he was now zooming toward the ground in flames.

Meggie looked back over her shoulder as she waddled toward the house. "If you cook dinner tonight, we'll talk."

The door shut, and Nick couldn't stop smiling for the next few hours.

Before smoothing down her tentlike sweater and skirt, Meg exhaled, her stomach feeling heavy, her heart, heavier.

What would they talk about? The weather?

She didn't think she could bring herself to refuse his love, and that scared her. She knew she was walking into another opportunity to have her spirits crushed, her heart beaten to mush.

No, she wouldn't give in to Nick's words. And even if he did fix every broken item around the house, she'd still refuse him. Her babies needed a real father, not someone who'd despise them because of their parentage. They needed someone who fancied love more than revenge.

But he never followed through with that revenge.

The inner-voice reminder sounded like something

Aunt Valentine would've said. Meg ignored the truth of it and walked out into the backyard, her hands propped on her aching back.

He sat by the lily pond, hovering over a spread-out blanket, a picnic basket clutched in his hands. He'd prepared an array of food, everything from a fruit salad surrounded by almonds to a plate of salmon garnished with parsley, tomatoes and onions. Cheese and crackers sat to one side, a rainbow of juices rested on a board next to the blanket. A heat lamp hovered over them, providing warmth against the fading sunset.

He gestured for her to take a seat and proceeded to serve her.

God, she hadn't been near him since the day he'd returned, and, even then, there hadn't been ample opportunity to enjoy his scent, his masculine power, in a relaxed state. Without being obvious, she ran her gaze over his dark-wheat hair, the slight curls of a needed haircut. The faint stubble that scratched his hard jawline. The cleft in his chin.

Being out here with him, under the colors of a setting sun, was crazy. It was as if he'd instructed Mother Nature to do his bidding, to make their surroundings as peaceful and seductive as possible.

It reminded her of the good days, before they'd shared secrets. And he was using the memories to his advantage, damn him.

He handed her a large pillow, and she tucked it behind her back, grateful for his attention to detail. "So where do we start?" she asked.

There. All business.

"You're not wearing your ring," he said.

She almost winced at his wounded tone. "My fingers are swollen."

"Oh." A pause. "Maybe I should come right out with what you want to hear."

"If it helps." Ouch. Why was she being so difficult when it was obvious that he was sincere?

He ignored her stubbornness. "I admit you were right about everything. I used Spencer...Chad...as a scapegoat to cushion my anger. I blamed my problems on others when I couldn't deal with the bigger issues myself. Yes, Chad ruined my life here in Kane's Crossing, but it wasn't his fault that I ended up in all those foster homes, some worse than others. It's time to let go of the past. And—" he sat on the blanket "—you helped me to realize it."

She shifted, not only because his proximity unsettled her, but because her back was aching something fierce. "I've got a confession, too."

"You don't have to say anything, Meggie."

"Yes, I do."

From the way he was watching her, she could tell he would gladly take on all her burdens, would fight all her battles. But, the best thing was, he'd given her the strength again to fight the battles herself.

How could she not love a man like Nick Cassidy?

"You shouldn't be apologizing to me when I owe you forgiveness. When Chad came back to town, I was going to lie to him. I was going to tell him that these babies were yours, not his."

"And I blew it by coming back."

She managed a smile. Of their own accord, she felt her fingers reaching out to stroke the stubble on his face. He leaned into her touch and, realizing what she'd done, she snatched back her hand.

His own grin remained, steady and true.

"Hardly, Nick. The point is, I was going to do what

you did, and I'd accused you of so many ugly things
before ordering you out of my life. I forgave you for
the way you felt a long time ago, but I couldn't come
to terms with the sense of betrayal.''

"Can you ever?''

She couldn't believe that tough Nick Cassidy would
seem so vulnerable, with his heart locked in his eyes
like an azure gemstone. He was still guarding those
priceless feelings, and rightly so.

"I don't know," she answered, hating the need to
be truthful.

The bulk of his shoulders tightened, and she knew
she'd hurt him again.

He looked away. "You can smell magnolias on the
wind.''

"Yes.'' Aunt Valentine had loved Nick as if he were
her own son. She would've wanted them together.

The miracle is in forgiveness.

Did she have that capacity? Could she be a bigger
person than she'd even been and reach out to Nick,
turning her back on the past to forge a new future?

Nick gently took her hand and led it to his flannel-
covered heart. "You'll always be my wife.''

She felt the *thump, thump* beneath her palm. How
many beats would it take for her to come to her senses,
backing away from this dizzy sense of love? She
wasn't even sure she wanted to deny him anymore.

"If you have any more secrets, tell me now, Nick
Cassidy.''

His lack of words scared her. Then he grinned, trans-
forming his face from sadness to utter joy. "Sorry.
Can't think of any.''

His smile made her light-headed, controlled by hormones and happiness. "Are you trying to make my life boring?"

"Wouldn't think of it," he murmured, stretching closer to her.

Their lips were inches apart, an electric sensation hovering through the space between, making her mouth tingle with the need to touch his.

A sharp pain tore through her, and she felt a gush of moisture between her legs. She jerked away from him.

The backaches combined with her water breaking. Was it time? From what she'd read, she thought she might be ready to have her babies.

Nick rested a steady hand on her shoulder. "Are you okay?"

"I'm not sure. I think I'm in labor." The throb in her lower back had spread to her lower abdomen. In spite of the pillow behind her back, she was finding it hard to relax.

He'd stood, hands on hips, "Mr. Cool" having passed with the first rip of pain. "Maybe I should get the truck?"

The aching subsided, allowing her to think clearly. She peered at the untouched food. "Your picnic will go to waste."

He stared sidelong at her. "Let's get going."

After he ran upstairs to fetch her hospital bag, they were on their way to the county hospital, the agony creeping up on Meg on big monster claws.

They'd thrown him out of the delivery room. Actually thrown him out.

Nick leaned against the hospital lobby's soda machine, tapping his booted foot against the linoleum. He checked his watch again, thinking that Meggie had been in there for a pretty long time.

She'd looked so pale, so fragile with her slender-puffed figure and protruding tummy garbed in a blue hospital gown.

Between contractions, she'd smiled at him. "Don't worry. This'll be over in a snap. Legend has it that the women in my family—ooo-ooh."

Then she'd gone into some serious labor. And Nick had stood by, draped in his own sanitary scrubs, fists clenching as he realized there was nothing he could to do protect his Meggie.

He'd been too confused to know that everything wasn't going as smoothly as she'd predicted. They'd had to haul him out of the sterile room, explaining that Meggie needed a Cesarean section and all would be well.

He needed to punch something.

Oh. No. He didn't do that anymore. But he was so frustrated, he wasn't sure what to do.

For the millionth time, he went to the nurses' station to ask about Meggie's progress.

"She's fine, sir. Why don't you have a seat?" said the efficient-looking guardian of death behind the counter.

He backed away, agitated as hell.

"Nick."

Rachel Shane rushed up to him, dressed in her ER scrubs. "I heard Meg went into labor."

He grabbed her arms, apologizing when she opened her mouth in shock. "You're a nurse. Can you find out what's happening?"

He caught her up with previous events, and she went charging into the delivery room, all fire and vinegar.

Time spun by as he waited for news. Finally, Rachel emerged from the hallway. "Just a C-section, Nick. Nothing to worry about."

"Aren't they cutting her open?"

Rachel rolled her eyes. "Relax, would you? She's had the kids. If you're willing, you're the proud papa of a healthy boy and girl. Cute as wailing buttons, too."

Nick's knees turned to jelly, and he thumped into a chair. He was a daddy.

And he'd be the best father he could, making sure he avoided the example set by his own natural parents. "When can I see them?"

"Do you want to wait until Meg comes out of recovery? She'll be an hour or so."

Rachel must've recognized the anticipation on his face, so she disappeared, grinning at him.

When she returned, she cuddled two bundles wrapped in hospital blankets, eyes shut tightly against the bright lights. He had such a lump in his throat, he thought he'd cry. Now, Nick Cassidy had overcome a lot in these past few months; he could say all the mushy things he wanted to Meggie, but he still needed time to work on the crying part.

He leaned his cheek near one of their faces, hearing the child's contented breathing, smelling its baby-soft scent.

For the next hour he held them, kissing their smooth faces, stroking their pudgy skin, fingering their perfectly formed fingernails. Nick didn't even mind when a tear came to his eye.

Rachel led him to Meggie's hospital room after they finished with his wife. When he walked into the room, his heart jarred to a stop. She waited, propped up by a load of pillows, as patient as an angel, her cheeks pale with exertion, dark circles as faint as twilight around her eyes.

God, she was beautiful.

He stopped at the edge of the bed, bending down to lay both infants in her arms. "Good job, Mommy."

Her smile melted him with its intensity. She cuddled the children, much the same way he had, rubbing her face against the down of their heads.

Meggie peered up at him from between her two children. "I love you so much."

He kissed all of them, his whole family, wondering what he'd done to earn this. "I love you, too."

Later, when they asked him to sign the birth certificate, he signed his name where it said "Father."

As the pen slid easily over the paper, he felt a sense of indescribable fulfillment. A real father protected his children, especially if the biological sperm donor was as unfit as Chad Spencer. By signing this certificate, he'd guarantee that Chad would never use the twins against Meggie or himself.

He would always be their protector.

When he handed the clipboard back to the nurse, his eyes locked on to Meggie's. Her gaze felt as warm as summer rain, as pulse-pounding as a sixteen-year marathon of uncertainty and ultimate victory.

She reached out to him, and he went to her, kissing her wrist, resting his head against her arm, the softness of one twin's baby blanket nipping his cheek.

They fell asleep, warmed by each other's comfort.

Epilogue

Five months later

There was nothing as stirring as Cutter's Hill basking under the glow of summer.

Meg smiled. Nothing, of course, except the sight of Nick watching the sun glimmering on Cutter's Lake, the twins cuddled in his arms as if they'd been born to be there.

Valerie and Jacob huddled against Nick's broad chest, their eyes darting from grass to tree, fists waving in the air as their father chuckled at them.

Content, Meg sat on the blanket, packing baby toys and tools back into their respective bags. Her shirt felt tighter over her stomach, her shorts felt snugger over her hips and thighs with every movement. She frowned, wondering if her daily exercise hour and walking with the twins in their strollers would ever yield any results. She couldn't wait to feel undoughlike again.

Nick always told her it didn't matter, that he loved every curve of her. He'd even made her feel that way back when she was pregnant. As if she'd been the most desirable woman in the world, looking like a hot air balloon.

Nick turned around, the twins drifting off to sleep in each arm. Gingerly, he stepped over to Meg, who helped him tuck Valerie and Jacob into their individual carry cradles.

Meg and Nick both plopped down onto the blanket, unable to take their eyes off their children.

Nick whispered, "Sam's going to reel from shock when he sees the kids."

Meg knew how excited Nick was about having his foster brother move back to Kane's Crossing. Their reunion wasn't under the best of circumstances—Sam had told Nick he needed to escape the house he and his beloved wife had lived in—but the brothers were determined to get reacquainted.

"You're the perfect dad," Meg said. "But who would've known? When you came back to me, you looked like you were ready to tear up Kane's Crossing."

She remembered the first time she'd seen Nick as an adult—one who'd grown up pretty darned good at that—hair windblown, dressed entirely in gunslinger-dark colors. He'd changed her life for the better, and her love for him grew into infinity.

He even had her believing that she could make things right with her parents. She'd received an answer to the birth announcement she'd sent. For the first time, she had hope that they'd love her again.

"You should've known I'd be back," he said.

Meg leaned against his chest, batting her eyelashes up at him.

Full circle. It always came back to the day on Cutter's Hill when she'd asked him if he loved her.

He looked into her eyes, and she remembered the shock on his fourteen-year-old face when she'd blurted the question so many years ago.

He paused, then smiled. "I love you, Meggie Cassidy."

Nick leaned to smooth a kiss over her lips. She'd never lose the thrill of his touch; each caress felt new, with the spark of that first contact, hot and electric.

As he pulled back, Meg saw the fulfilled dreams in Nick's eyes, the dance of magnolia blossoms, sunsets and July moons.

He smiled, and there was no yearning in his gaze, no cry for justice. Just an extraordinary love for his family.

The miracle is in forgiveness.

Thank goodness they'd done their forgiving. It was time to really start living.

*   *   *   *   *

Coming soon from
Silhouette Special Edition,
watch for the next sizzling installment in

KANE'S CROSSING.

Will a star-crossed romance ignite
between Sheriff Sam Reno and
the sassy town socialite?
Find out in

HIS ARCH ENEMY'S DAUGHTER

by Crystal Green in March 2002!

Turn the page for a sneak preview...

Chapter One

Ashlyn Spencer was in a real fix this time.

"Emma, why don't you put away that shotgun?" she asked while backing out of the insect-buzzed porch light and into the shadows. She felt erased, almost safe in the darkness cast by Mrs. Trainor's roof.

The older woman's outline didn't budge from the screened window. "I'll be darned if you play any April Fool's jokes on Trainor property, Miss Spencer. You, me and my sawed-off friend will wait right here until the sheriff comes."

Ashlyn wanted to speak up in her defense, to tell Emma that she wasn't playing any pranks tonight— hadn't played any for a long time now. In fact, this bundle of crisp one-hundred-dollar bills she held in her hand was sticking to her palms with the urgency of cats clinging to a curtain for safety.

Right about now, they were all victims of worst-case scenario shotgun nightmares.

"Emma, I—"

A deep voice rumbled over her protestations. "Lower your gun, Emma."

Ashlyn could hear the woman's sigh of relief, even through a window screen meshed with Kentucky flies and a trace of dandelion down.

The sheriff and his boots thumped their way up the stairs, onto the porch. "You put that firearm away, Emma?"

A heavy clicking sound from behind the older woman's door made Ashlyn start from her hiding place. Was Emma Trainor cocking the gun?

Ashlyn jolted backward and smashed right into the new sheriff, his chest as broad and hard as a wall. Not literally, but it felt like so many hard bricks piled together—enough to make her see stars.

Sam Reno had returned to town.

The same man who'd been the object of Ashlyn's star-in-the-eyes fantasies, her *Teen Beat* dreams.

She gulped and subtly tried to stand in back of him, just in case Emma was aiming in her direction.

The other woman stepped onto the porch, and Ashlyn felt her face heat up when she realized that the "click" had merely been the screen door opening.

Emma nodded to the sheriff. "Thanks for answering so fast. I heard an intruder out here and found Ashlyn Spencer lurking around my door."

Ashlyn hid her hands behind her back, hoping no one had seen the money, hoping no one would suspect that she was up to *good* for a change.

Sheriff Reno placed his hands on his lean hips, his silhouette dark against the moon's silver light. "You're going to get someone killed with your weaponry, Emma. Now, I know better than anyone that you want your protection, but pumping bullets into the town socialite won't rid the world of evil. I'd hate to take you in for that.''

Ashlyn felt the sheriff shoot her a glance, but she bit her tongue, determined to let them think what they would about her reasons for being here.

Emma stuck her fists in the pockets of her oversized jeans. ''Sorry, Sam. I didn't even have a gun. Had to use a fire poker. The girl scared me, sneaking around like she was, creaking my porch boards.''

Truth be told, Ashlyn wished she hadn't frightened Mrs. Trainor. The woman had suffered enough pain in her life, what, with her husband dying in the same factory accident that had killed Sam Reno's own father. And she felt partly responsible, too, because it was her family's factory. Her family's responsibility—one that they'd never owned up to.

Sheriff Reno took a step forward into the faint porch light, affording Ashlyn a better vantage point.

He had the corded strength of a Remington sculpture, all rough edges and darkness. His clipped brown hair barely brushed his jacket collar, and it was longer on top, falling to just above his stern brow. The fullness of his lower lip gave her heart a lurch, and it wasn't because he was frowning.

He shook his head, his voice as low and dry as an endless stretch of desert road. ''Well, I guess you can't do a whole lot of damage with a phantom arsenal.''

A few more steps brought him closer to Emma. Softly, he asked, ''How're you doing?''

The older woman's lips trembled, and Ashlyn had to avert her glance.

"As well as can be expected. Janey's still in the hospital, for as long as the money'll keep her there."

Ashlyn tightened her grip on the hundred-dollar bills and looked up.

Sam Reno cupped his long fingers under the woman's jaw, making Ashlyn's throat ache. His touch was so gentle, so sympathetic, like a physical connection between two survivors who'd lost everything.

She felt invisible, surrounded by the darkness of cave walls, blocking her from the rest of humanity. Dank, lonely, so dark...

Ashlyn washed her mind of those thoughts. She needed to forget about the cave, about the scared seven-year-old girl who'd lived under the banner of town disapproval for so long.

But how could she forget that her family had caused such pain?

Unthinkingly, she cleared her throat, wanting to slap herself when it broke the moment between Emma and the sheriff. He turned to her, a glower of displeasure clearly marking his face.

"What the hell were you doing creeping around here in the dead of night?" he asked.

She tried to shine her most innocent smile, but it didn't quite hold. "I'll have to plead the fifth on that."

His gaze had focused on her hands, folded behind her back very suspiciously. "Drop it." His fingers had tensed near his holster, the one with the gun in it.

Ashlyn reluctantly dropped the wad of money and held her hands in the air, shrugging as she did so. "Whoops."

He stepped near her, brushing her sweater with his jacket as he ambled by. She shivered, probably because the April night had a sudden warm thrill to it.

He held up the money. "This should be an interesting explanation."

Emma Trainor's jaw almost hit the floor boards. Why was she so shocked? Was it so unthinkable that Ashlyn would want to help someone in their time of need?

Well, now she'd have to explain. Unless, of course, she desired an all-expense-paid trip to the sheriff's office.

Actually, she thought, if Sheriff Sam was doing the driving, it didn't sound all that bad....